BEYOND TEMPTATION

To Kim,
Give in to temptation.
Always.

Kit Rocha

kit rocha

Beyond Temptation

Originally published in the MARKED anthology

Edited by Sasha Knight

ISBN-13: 978-1499673111
ISBN-10: 1499673116

For Lauren Dane and Vivian Arend.

Thank you both for joining us
in this mad, epic adventure. Much love.

R EVENGE WAS ADDICTIVE.

Crouched on the roof of an abandoned warehouse, Noah snapped his lighter open and shut, the one nervous habit he allowed himself. He'd given up cigarettes years ago, but sometimes he felt the urge, especially on nights like this. Nights when justice was playing out before him, set into motion by a few righteous keystrokes.

Shadows moved across the street, figures slipping through the darkness, silent as ghosts. He knew they were coming, and he still almost missed them. One dark blur knelt in front of the shop door and slipped something from his pocket while two more melted into the alleys on either side, their shoes soundless on the cracked, gravel-strewn asphalt.

Eden trained their hitmen well. Not that they usually wasted an entire Special Tasks squad rounding up criminals from outside the walls—everyone in the sectors was a criminal, at least in the minds of the fancy folks in Eden—but sometimes they made an exception. Sometimes you could *make* them make an exception.

Boots thumped lightly on the roof behind him, a split second before a low whisper broke the silence. "Did I miss the show?"

Noah recognized the voice. Brendan Donnelly, one of the most dangerous men in Sector Four, and not only because its leader depended on him. Bren wore the ink of the O'Kane gang now, but he'd come from Eden, from a Special Tasks squad.

Not a man to underestimate. "I'm impressed you knew there was going to be a show."

"Got a tip from an old friend." Bren crouched beside him and peered down at the alley. "Don't worry. It took me a while to link it back to you."

Across the street, the men were already carrying boxes out of the house. Fast. Silent. They piled them into the back of the electric vehicle in front of the shop, box after box of useless evidence. They undoubtedly hoped to figure out how some greedy sector seamstress had managed to manufacture the credits they used inside the shining walls of their utopian city.

It would take them years to realize she hadn't. It had taken Bren less than twenty-four hours. "What gave me away?"

"What else?" Bren flashed him a knowing look, then nodded down to the shop. "Emma apprenticed with her before coming to the Broken Circle, didn't she?"

Jaw clenched, Noah watched them drag the woman out into the street and shove her into the back of the truck. He'd paid her more than enough to keep Emma in goddamn luxury, and she'd pocketed it and put the girl to work. "She wasn't supposed to be an apprentice. She was supposed to be safe until the heat from Sector Five died down."

"I thought that might be how it was," Bren said flatly.

"How much did she take you for?"

More money than someone like her could have expected to see in a lifetime, but that wasn't why he'd set her up for such a terrifying fall. Emma had split, and Clara Danforth, facing the loss of those monthly payments, had gone for a payday. "Remember when you told me Emma was an O'Kane, and I didn't believe you?"

"I do."

"Fifty thousand." In the street below, the car pulled away. The rest of the squad melted into the shadows, undoubtedly to find their own way back to Eden's gates. No one stayed in the grimy hell of the sectors longer than they had to. "That was how much I paid for Emma and the farmer she'd supposedly fallen in love with to get into one of the mountain communities. She was supposed to be gone. She was supposed to be *safe*."

Bren swore, quiet and vicious. "That sucks."

More than Bren would ever know. The money was nothing. Unlike the seamstress, Noah really could make credits appear from thin air. Not that he'd used those for Emma's fresh start—that had been cash, almost everything he had left, and he'd sent it along with a clean conscience and a numb heart. It wasn't the end to the story he'd wanted, but it was the one he'd promised her brother. Emma was safe, happy, and nothing else could matter.

Except he'd fucked that up, too.

Straightening, Noah shoved his lighter into his pocket. "I guess your boss probably wants to see me."

"Figured you'd want to meet with him." Another penetrating look. "More importantly, I thought you'd want to see Emma."

He did, and wanting felt awkward after so many years of numbness. He didn't have room for feelings or desires. Emma had the potential to be a fatal distraction—and if the wrong people realized just how much she distracted him, he wouldn't be the one to suffer the consequences.

5

But he had to know she was okay. Not a want. A *need.* "Yeah. I'd like to see her."

"Then come on." Bren rose, casting one last look down at the silent, still street. "Show's over, anyways."

It hadn't been much of one, and that was how Noah preferred it. Quiet. Efficient. No way to trace it back to him—unless you had contacts inside Eden and knew his weakness.

He couldn't afford to have one, not if he planned to take down the man who had murdered Emma's brother and destroyed Noah's life. Which meant getting Emma out of the sectors or out of his system. Either worked, because one way or another, that chink in his armor had to be patched, or they'd both end up dead.

Bren was already moving toward the fire escape, so Noah followed, doing his best to ignore the wobbly iron and the rust. The whole thing felt fragile enough to crumble under their boots, so jumping the last five feet to the chipped pavement was almost a relief.

At least the buildings in this corner of the sectors were solid, not the leaning, rickety death traps he was used to in Three. Dallas O'Kane kept Sector Four relatively well-maintained—and under his absolute control.

No wonder he'd somehow known about the raid.

The closer they drew to the O'Kane compound, the cleaner everything got. No more cluttered alleyways or figures congregating in the shadows. The streets were well-lit, and it was easy to follow the noise and crowds to the very edge of Dallas O'Kane's personal empire.

Bren slowed near a sprawling brick building. Its façade was lit up, and thumping music spilled out of the barred windows and door. "Welcome to the Broken Circle."

Noah tried to reply, but a group of drunks shoved through the doors, and he got his first glimpse of the stage—and the person dancing on it.

Sweet little Emmaline Cibulski was all grown up.

It was a truth he'd never expected to face, not after

6

three years of trying to forget she ever existed. He'd written a happy ending for her in his mind, one where she still looked like the nineteen-year-old girl he'd bundled out of Sector Five in the middle of the night. One where she was blonde, pink-cheeked from the cool mountain air, and probably pregnant with her second baby by that nice, boring-as-fuck farmer, living a nice, boring-as-fuck life.

The woman dominating the stage of the Broken Circle wasn't nineteen. She wasn't innocent. And she sure as fuck wasn't boring.

Music washed over Noah as he slipped through the door, a rough bass line that pounded in time with his heart as Emma gripped the hilts of the knives strapped to her sleek thighs and circled her hips with a raw, knowing sexuality that had Noah's dick half-hard already.

Emma was stripping at the most infamous bar in all eight sectors, a fact that would have been crazy enough all on its own. But tattoos curled around her wrists, cuffs that stretched from the tops of her hands halfway to her elbows, a sight only slightly less infamous than the bar. Members of Dallas's gang wore those cuffs, inescapable proof that she really *had* joined up with the O'Kanes.

Appreciative noises rose from the crowd as Emma slipped the sharp end of one blade under her shirt, slicing the tight black cotton right down the middle. It pulled away, baring her breasts—and the taut pink tips of her nipples.

The knife fell from her fingers with a clatter, and she jerked the cotton together with a wicked grin. Pleas and groans of disappointment rose from the crowd in equal measure, and she peeled the shirt open again, this time letting it slide off her shoulders to the floor.

Half-hard? How optimistic. Noah was a raging pervert, rock-hard and transfixed by her gorgeous tits—not to mention the seductive twist of her hips. Somehow, *somehow*, he had to remember that those tits and hips belonged to Cib's baby sister, and that he'd made a

7

promise.

Keep her safe. Get her out of the sectors, or out of his system.

Both were looking less possible by the minute.

"Solid show, Em."

"Thanks." Emma dropped her knives and sheaths on the dressing table and slid her arms into her robe. The brushed satin stroked her skin like a lover, and she shivered as she drew her hair up into a loose knot.

Dancing was a rush, all right, the kind that kicked her senses and her adrenaline into overdrive, same as a fight. Sometimes, afterwards, all she wanted to do was *fuck*.

"Ladies." Dallas's familiar voice rumbled through the dressing room, and half the dancers rushed across the floor to fawn over him.

Emma watched him in the mirror instead. He was a big man, but he moved with absolute grace—the kind of self-assurance that came from owning everything around him, probably. From the top of his dark head to the tips of his worn boots, Dallas O'Kane was in charge. No questions asked.

His gaze met hers in the mirror, and Dallas patted one of the dancers on the hip before raising his voice above the noise. "Em, darling, I need a word. Upstairs."

She spun on her stool. "In your office?"

"Conference room." He tilted his head and seemed to consider. "You might want to get dressed first."

There went any chance he'd come to fetch her because tonight was the night he and Lex were finally going to rock her world. Emma kept her voice even as she rose and reached for her pants. "Something wrong?"

The other dancers were watching now, quiet and nervous. None of the other girls backstage tonight were family, and whatever Dallas had to say, it was clear he didn't plan to share it with outsiders. "Nothing to worry about. Just a little O'Kane business."

Emma threw off her robe and dressed quickly. "Break a leg out there tonight, girls." She snatched up her bag and followed Dallas through the curtain, out into the back hall.

He didn't speak until they reached the stairs, but the words were enough to make her stumble mid-stride. "Noah Lennox is upstairs."

Shock rendered her tongue thick. "Noah's *here?*"

Dallas caught her arm and steadied her. "In the conference room, talking to Lex. But before you see him, I wanted to talk to *you.*"

Noah Lennox. He was the only remaining link to her past, a past full of struggle and pain and loss. The last time she'd seen him, he'd dropped her off on a back street in Sector Four in the middle of the night. No promises to come back for her, nothing. She'd missed him horribly for weeks, and then hated him just as intensely for leaving her.

She shouldn't have wanted to see him, but she did. So much her throat ached.

"Hey, darling." Dallas's fingers brushed her chin before he tilted her face up. "If you don't want to look at him, we'll spin right back around and that'll be it."

She shook herself and tried for a smile. "It's not that. I'm surprised, is all. I haven't seen him in four years."

"Well, this was inevitable. He's got skills I need, and I have resources he can use." Dallas dropped his hand but held her gaze. "I need to know if you can handle that."

Dallas wanted him around, of course—a hacker with Noah's abilities was invaluable—but something else lurked beneath the words. A question, but also a warning. "What are you saying?"

Exhaling, Dallas wrapped his fingers around her wrist—and her ink. "I'm saying you're an O'Kane. We need him, bad. But you're not a whore and you're not a prize, and I need to know you understand. Lex and I will ask a lot of you, but never that."

He could, though. There was no one to stop him, and precious few who would even try. In Sector Four, Dallas was the law.

It made his consideration that much more meaningful. Emma leaned up and kissed his cheek. "Any other time, I might do it. But not with Noah. He was my brother's best friend, and he saved my life. He deserves better than getting played."

Dallas snorted and smacked her ass, urging her up the stairs. "If he can get me the intel I need, I'll bury him in all the willing pussy he wants. No playing."

Noah had never flaunted his women in front of Emma, but she knew what he was into. "He likes 'em dirty," she muttered as she started for the second floor. "*Really* dirty."

"Does he, now?"

Again, a question hovered just under the words. "Observation, not firsthand experience."

"Mm-hmm." When they reached the landing, he slung an arm around her shoulders. "Once you're done chatting with him, we'll spin him by tonight's afterparty. Give him a taste of what we can offer. If he likes dirty ladies, I'll own his ass."

Emma elbowed him in the ribs, then freed herself from his embrace and took a deep breath before slipping into the conference room.

Noah looked the same. A little rough, like he'd had a bad couple of days, but still *Noah*, who was always sweet and warm, just for her. The same red hair and ginger beard, the same broad shoulders that could block out the world if she needed them to.

Christ, she'd missed him.

She was halfway across the conference room before she caught herself and stopped. "Noah."

He stared at her, his gaze flickering across her face, as if cataloging all the things about her that had changed.

"Emmy."

Her lips trembled into a smile, and she pressed her fingers to them. "I thought I'd never see you again."

"I didn't know you were still here, in the sectors. I thought—" He cleared his throat and lifted his right arm. He'd done it a hundred times before, inviting her to duck under it for a hug while he ruffled her hair and teased her. But before she could move, his arm fell to his side again, and he looked away. "She told me you'd left. If I'd known the truth, I would have come to get you. I would have taken you somewhere safe."

"I did leave. I came here." *Fuck it.* Emma wrapped her arms around his neck in a firm hug. "You look so damn good."

He stiffened against her, then slid one arm around her waist in an awkward embrace. "You look...grown up."

She bit her lip to hold in a laugh. "Four years'll do that."

"I guess it will." He skated a hand lightly up her back until he reached her arm and tugged it away from his neck to examine her O'Kane ink. The coolness in his gaze melted into regret. "This is the life I was trying to keep you out of."

God only knew what he thought of Sector Four—and the O'Kanes. "No, this is—it's nothing like Sector Five here. Dallas isn't Mac Fleming."

"He moves booze instead of drugs," Noah agreed, rubbing his thumb over the O'Kane logo. "I guess it's a step up. But I wanted to get you out. To the mountains, like Cib used to dream about."

She jerked her hand away. "I wasn't talking business. People here look out for each other."

Noah studied her face in tense silence before lowering his voice. "I've read Eden's files on Dallas O'Kane and his inner circle. Some of these bastards could give Mac Fleming nightmares. If you're scared—"

"Oh, Jesus." Emma stood there, torn between laughing and crying. "I'm not a hostage, Noah. This is my family."

No comprehension in his eyes. He didn't believe her—or *couldn't*—though he didn't say so. Instead, he took a step back and shoved his hands into his pockets. "You're happy?"

She couldn't answer, because he wouldn't believe that, either. "Let me show you. Stay for a little while?"

"Okay."

"Okay?"

He shrugged and looked away. "I'll stay. For the night, at least. O'Kane's woman invited me to some party."

Every time she'd allowed herself to imagine reuniting with Noah, the fantasy had been different. Sweet or sexy, happy or even a bit sad. Bittersweet. But nothing had prepared her for this awkwardness, the chasm between them that seemed to widen with every passing moment.

She had no idea what to say to him.

They stared at each other forever, tense and miserable. Then he bit off a curse and turned away. "I didn't know," he snarled, the words so low and furious she barely understood them. "I didn't know I'd have to do this again."

"Noah." Her clumsiness melted, and she reached for him, smoothing her hands over the knotted muscles of his shoulders.

He shuddered under her touch. "You have no idea, Emmy. No goddamn *clue* how bad I was when you knew me, and how much worse I am now."

"Come on," she whispered. "That isn't true."

Laughter sliced out of him, harsh and broken. "Don't get any romantic ideas about me. I've always been a criminal."

It made her sound like a foolish little girl, and she'd always prided herself on being pragmatic. Just because she was an artist didn't mean she was a dreamer, floating along with her head in the clouds.

Emma stepped back. "Why did you come here?"

"To make sure you were okay. And because O'Kane can help me."

"Help you with what?"

He turned to stare out the window, giving her a glimpse of his hard profile and clenched jaw. "Take down Mac Fleming. Even if I have to go down with him."

Emma shivered. "If you set Fleming on fire, Dallas wouldn't piss on him to put it out. But it's not worth—" She touched Noah's arm. "Look at me, damn it."

When he did, it hurt worse. He looked tired, used up, like there was nothing good left inside him. Only revenge.

It made her words ring hollow, even to her own ears. "It's not worth dying over."

Noah raised his hand to stroke one of the blonde streaks of hair back from her face. His fingers followed it down to her bare shoulder, where he traced the outline of one tattoo. "I'm fucking this up. If I'd known I'd be seeing you again, I would have held on a little harder."

The detached regret scared her most of all, as if he was already gone in every way that mattered. Her heart pounding, she mirrored his movement, testing the solid strength of his neck and shoulder beneath his shirt.

He'd saved her once. It wouldn't be right to let him drift away like this, not if she could help it.

Emma leaned in, brushing her lips to the corner of his mouth.

Groaning, he plunged his fingers into her hair, tangling them up tight enough to hold her there, on the verge of a kiss. "Why?"

Nothing less than the truth. "Because you're here, and you're alive. And I missed you."

He closed his eyes. His mouth moved against hers—words, not a caress, though they felt the same. "I'm not good enough for you. I never was."

Once upon a time, he'd been one of the few stable things in her whole world. She'd loved him with all her young, naive heart, and with him this close, so close that his breath was hers too, that emotion fluttered anew in her belly.

Emma wrapped her hands around his upper arms. "Do you want to be good enough for me?"

His fist tightened, edging her head back. His parted lips brushed her chin, her jaw. "That's a question I've never let myself ask."

She'd experienced mind-bending pleasure, fallen into the spaces between naked, eager partners with zeal and joy. But none of it had ever made her tremble to her core, not like Noah's lips skating a path down her throat. "Then you must have known the answer would be yes."

"And damn me for it," he groaned, lifting his head to meet her gaze. "I'll hurt you. I won't want or mean to, but I'll do it. Mark my words, Emma."

"Shh." It would be worth it to show him—what belonging felt like, what home was, everything she hadn't been able to say as a shy nineteen-year-old with a desperate crush. "I know what this is, Noah. What it isn't. Just kiss me."

His mouth hovered over hers, so close his sigh ghosted across her lips like a promise. He relaxed his hand, fingers cupping the back of her head, and started to close the distance—

The door crashed open. "Keep it in your pants, Cibulski. We're all locked up downstairs, and that boy has an O'Kane party to get to."

She refused to jump away from Noah like a kid caught making out. "We're just catching up, Dallas."

"Uh-huh. Save it for the orgy." He grinned and vanished, leaving the door hanging open.

Both of Noah's eyebrows swept up. "Orgy, huh?"

"That's Dallas's version of the hard sell." She kissed Noah on the cheek. "His recruitment speech."

His expression finally cracked into a smile. "I bet it's effective."

The smile kindled the first glimmer of hope, and Emma slid her hand into his. "You can let me know in a few hours."

2

O'KANE HAD CALLED it an orgy.
He hadn't been exaggerating.

Only iron will kept Noah from shifting to relieve the uncomfortably tight fit of his jeans as he watched a couple fuck their way into the midst of a threesome that broke apart and reformed around them without losing momentum. No one seemed to care who the hands and mouths and tongues belonged to, as long as they kept touching in all the right places—and judging by the frequent squeals of pleasure, everyone knew which places were right.

It wasn't the first time he'd seen unchecked carnal indulgence play out before him, but it was the first time it had been accompanied by so much female enthusiasm. And so much laughter.

O'Kane's right-hand man sat beside Noah, squinting at him. "You gonna make it?"

"I think I'll pull through somehow," he replied blandly.

The man only nodded. Jasper McCray was a bastard with a dangerous reputation, and his looks fit it. He was decked out in leather, denim, and tattoos, complete with shaggy hair, a full beard, and a stern frown. In Sector Five, the woman seated between his legs would have been another accessory. She was dressed like one, in ruffled lingerie and expensive jewelry. She rested her cheek on Jasper's leg, and her eyelids drooped with sleepy pleasure when he teased his fingers through her hair. Absent-minded affection—something that just didn't happen in Five.

The girl—Noelle, he thought her name was—smiled suddenly, and Noah followed her gaze back to the open floor beyond the dais and nearly swallowed his tongue.

Emma had taken to dancing in one brightly lit spot. She was wearing the same shirt, a black scrap of nothing with tiny sleeves that left her shoulders bare, but she'd shed her jeans. Her panties had two ties on each side, one high on her hip and one low.

The ribbons hung down her thighs, silk brushing silk, as she tipped her head back and spun in a slow circle. Her tattoos cut bright, colorful paths across her skin, wrapping around her thighs and arms, climbing up her sides, the beautiful designs fitting the contours of her body to perfection.

She was a work of art, and he couldn't tear his gaze away.

Noelle sighed from her spot on the floor. "She's so beautiful."

Emma dropped to her knees and slipped her hands into her hair, gathering it high at her crown. She rolled her head forward this time, a slow tilt from one shoulder to the other, and when her gaze lifted, her eyes clashed with Noah's.

Then one hand crept out of her hair, down the side of her neck, and over her collarbone to toy with the top edge of her shirt.

Everything he'd told her in that damn conference room was still true. He didn't deserve her. He never had. And now he'd forgotten how to be human, how to deal with people instead of data, how to give a shit about anything except his revenge.

The need to protect her had exploded into his numb heart, the memory of a feeling that had once dominated his life so completely that even the echo hurt. Another echo was stirring, one he'd never wanted to acknowledge as real, one laced with guilt and loathing and shattered trust—

I see the way you look at her.

No, he'd never deserved her. But he'd wanted her— and now that feeling was smashing its way into the frozen wasteland inside him, so much more intense than a mere memory. Even at his lowest he'd never wanted this badly, his cock rock hard and his mind already imagining how her mouth would feel around it.

Innocence had never gotten him going. Not like this.

The black fabric dipped down, barely clinging to the hard peaks of Emma's nipples, then slid free to nestle beneath her breasts. His breath caught in his chest as he let his gaze linger on her curves, on the tight little buds he could almost taste.

Then she reached lower.

"Fuck me." The husky curse came from Lex, the brunette curled up in Dallas O'Kane's lap. "Are we gonna get a show tonight?"

Jesus *Christ*, Noah had forgotten the rest of them were even there. And he still couldn't look away, not with Emma's fingers headed toward the bit of fabric masquerading as underwear.

"Maybe I should help her," Noelle murmured, uncurling from her spot between Jasper's knees.

Noah had two seconds to imagine what that might mean—two filthy seconds his brain all too readily filled with an image of Emma astride Noelle's face, writhing her hips as Noelle licked and moaned—before Jasper twisted a hand in the girl's hair and tugged her back against the couch.

"Not this time," he told her, and he said it like his woman's tongue in Emma's pussy wasn't just possible, but a common fucking occurrence.

Dallas laughed and stroked a hand up Lex's thigh. "Look at the big eyes on him, love. One of you better warn Lennox about tangling with O'Kane women, or our little Emma's gonna eat him alive."

"No." Lex leaned closer, close enough for Noah to feel her breath on his skin as she stared into his eyes. "No, I think this one knows exactly what he wants."

Anyone with sense in their head could probably tell he wanted Emma, but there was something unsettling about Lex's gaze. It slid deeper, beneath his armor, beneath his skin. He'd read the file on her, too. It claimed she'd grown up in one of Sector Two's elite brothels, trained to read a man with a look and control him with a touch.

Both seemed chillingly possible, so he deflected. "Does any man ever know what he wants?"

"Know? Yes." She sat back and threaded her fingers through Dallas's hair. "Whether he admits it is a whole different question, honey."

Emma's voice twisting into a moan dragged his gaze back. She held her hand still and rocked her hips, gliding into her own touch.

Sweet *fuck.*

He pressed his fists to his thighs and watched her, trying to memorize the rhythm of her body, the sound of her voice. He wasn't the only one watching, but her eyes were on him, and when her mouth moved again, her lips silently formed his name.

He was going to spend the next twenty years dream-ing about this.

Then she stopped, a sudden, wicked smile curving her lips. She rose, stripped off her tangled shirt, and toyed with one beribboned tie at her hip as she walked toward the dais.

She stepped up onto it—and stopped right in front of him. The faint music playing in the room melted into something lower, heavier, and Emma eased onto his lap, her knees on either side of his legs.

He caught her hips, pinning them in place just above his. If she lowered them, they'd be fucking on this couch, probably while Dallas and Jas and their girlfriends stared on in fascination. "Emma."

"Noah." She cupped his face, her fingers stroking his cheeks, his jaw, his mouth.

Her tits were almost in his face. One tug and he could be licking them, sucking her nipples between his lips and finding out just how many noises she could make. He could barely remember why he wasn't already doing it.

"Yes," she whispered, circling her hips. When he loosened his grip a little, she did it again, dipping and swaying above him before dropping low enough to grind against his dick through his pants.

He jerked his gaze from her chest, but there was nowhere safe to look. Dallas had his hand under Lex's skirt while he murmured something against her ear, and Noelle was tugging at Jasper's zipper and giving him big, entreating eyes. "Please let me, please."

"Will you be good?" Jasper rumbled.

"Yes. You were right." Noelle nuzzled his knee with a husky laugh. "I don't think Emma needs any help tonight."

"Mmm." He released her hand and her head with a nod. "Behave, and maybe you can help her, after all."

Emma barely seemed to hear—or she just didn't care. She was staring at his mouth, her body trembling so close, so damn *close*—

Letting go had never been so literal. He eased his grip, and she settled against him, her hips straddling his aching cock, her bare breasts crushed against his shirt, her mouth finding his as if kissing her had always been inevitable.

Maybe it had been.

Her lips were sweet, soft, at odds with her nails digging in to his arm, sharp and rough. That was Emma now, he realized—as sweet as always, but with a filthy edge, one that had her riding him like he was already inside her.

He could be inside her.

The thought had barely formed when Dallas snorted. "So much for that. Get a room, Cibulski."

She tossed her head back and pinned her leader with a challenging look. "You're the one who told me to bring him."

"My miscalculation." Dallas swatted Emma's hip. "Don't get me wrong, girl. I'm sure it'd entertain the hell out of us to watch you two fuck, but Lex'll pout if you don't even notice she's here. You just remember what I said."

"Trust me, Dallas." She slid off Noah's lap and tugged him to his feet. "You're the last thing I'm thinking about right now."

O'Kane laughed. "Fuck you too, love."

Emma dragged Noah behind her. She hopped off the stage and plowed toward the door without bothering to haul her clothes back into place, as if it couldn't possibly matter. And since most of the people in the room were varying degrees of naked, maybe it didn't.

She pulled him through the door, into the dark hallway. "If they didn't give you a room yet, we can go to mine."

Guilt tried to wiggle through his body's throbbing need. He'd never said he was staying beyond the night, and she hadn't asked. She still wasn't asking, just making assumptions that he should correct. But if he did...

He could taste her mouth on his tongue. He wanted to taste other parts of her. He wanted to fall into her and not worry about tomorrow.

He wanted her to keep talking like she wanted him to stay, instead of assuring him it didn't matter either way.

Emmaline Cibulski had needed his protection. This

confident, dangerous O'Kane woman could take care of herself—and the ink around her wrists would keep her safer than Noah ever could. That was what he told himself, anyway, as he slid a hand around her waist and pressed his lips to her ear. "Take me to your bed."

Ushering Noah into the darkness of her room fulfilled a fantasy Emma thought had died. She'd been sheltered for the longest time, unable to fantasize about anything but the vaguest of details—soft kisses, gentle words, his hand sliding down her body. And none of those things fit with an O'Kane woman, tough and self-assured. They were the desires of an innocent.

They came back to life here, now, as her hand trembled in his. "Hang on. I'll get the light." Any excuse to pull free so he couldn't feel her shaking.

She flicked on the lamp closest to the door, and it flooded the room with a low, gentle glow. She watched as Noah looked around, his gaze jumping from one object to another as if building a mental catalog before sweeping upward.

He smiled. "Your ceiling's blue."

The first thing she always did was paint her ceiling. "I like it that way."

"I remember," he murmured, still staring. "One year Cib and I damn near took the sector apart before your birthday, trying to find enough blue paint to get the job done, but my contact fell through. Good thing I found those pencils at the last minute."

He'd also found someone to make her a pad of sketch paper, the thick kind with the fibers she could still feel under her fingertips. But the charcoal pencils—*that* had been the prize. Not the bits of burned wood she normally used, but real pencils of varying hardness, wrapped in slick paper with a thread on the side she could pull when she needed to peel more away.

Her eighteenth birthday. It had been a time of jubilant celebration, the three of them so happy, completely oblivious to the fact that, within a single short year, her brother would be dead.

She swallowed hard. "I still have them, you know. The pencils. They're just nubs now." And she could never bring herself to use up that last bit of charcoal.

His gaze dropped back to her body, tracing the edges of one of her tattoos. "I guess you found a new way to make art."

"I didn't do any of these." Emma reached down to trace the vine of roses climbing the outside of her right thigh. "I designed this one, though."

Noah crouched in front of her, so close she could feel the warmth of his breath as his fingertip followed after hers. "It's beautiful."

So close. She sank her fingers into his hair and pulled. He smiled and kept touching her, curling his hand around the back of her thigh to slide down to her knee and up again.

Emma let go of him and untied another ribbon on her panties as she backed slowly toward the bed. "Is this a little more your speed? All alone instead of surrounded by people?"

He shrugged. "I'm sure it's more fun when you're one of them and you know the rules. But even if I wanted to, I'm not stupid enough to get too friendly with a woman who belongs to Dallas O'Kane or Jasper McCray."

"Lex doesn't belong to Dallas—they belong to each other. Same with Jas and Noelle."

He paused and tilted his head to one side. "That's always been the talk, but when you've lived in a place like Five, you wonder how much is just that—talk."

"Mmm." All the more reason for him to stick around and see for himself. But Emma held her tongue and forgot all about it when the backs of her legs hit her bed. She dropped her panties and sank to the mattress.

Holding her gaze, Noah rose and gripped the hem of his shirt, teasing her with the possibility of bare skin. "Does your room have rules?"

Her palms itched to explore, and she curled her hands into fists at her sides. "Just the same ones we have everywhere else. If everybody says yes, anything goes."

His arms flexed as he hauled his shirt over his head and let it fall. "Then touch me."

Touch him? He may as well have asked her to touch some priceless pre-Flare sculpture. The lines were the same, chiseled and perfect, but carved from muscle instead of stone. Alive and responsive.

Emma came to her knees. She traced the hard swell of one pectoral, grazed his nipple, and molded her hand to his shoulder. "You're beautiful." His skin was bare, unadorned, but she could already see the art beneath it, the places where she'd lay ink.

His head tilted back, and he swallowed. "I'm out of practice," he said roughly. "I haven't had a lot of time for...affection lately."

"No?" That was a shame. A body like his should be celebrated—tasted and stroked and licked and sketched, committed to memory in every sense that existed.

He choked on a laugh and lifted a hand to cover hers. "I live in an underground bunker. Not a lot of guests."

"Ah." Emma let her fingers roam, following the trail of hair that narrowed over his stomach and disappeared into his jeans. She unbuckled his belt slowly, giving him time to stop her.

His breathing sped, but he didn't move until she'd tugged open the button on his fly and was reaching for the zipper. He closed his hand around her wrist, fingers big and broad but careful. "I keep waiting for you to disappear. Nothing I want this much could be real."

As if she had to be some kind of dream. Emma's cheeks heated. "I'm not going anywhere, Noah." She tugged her hand free and pulled his zipper down, the soft rasp shivering up her spine. "I'm right where I want to be."

"I know." The words held an edge of sadness, but he covered it in the next moment by sliding his fingers deep into her hair. "I don't know if I have the willpower to let you put your mouth on me. I won't last, not tonight."

It was intoxicating, the thought that he could want her that hard, that much. "So? Come in my mouth, and then show me all the things you've wanted to do to me."

Noah groaned, his fingers tightening until her scalp tingled. "That is a filthy fucking suggestion."

"Delicate O'Kanes don't exist." Emma settled to the mattress, easing his pants down as she went. His cock sprang free, erect and eager, and she took a moment to explore its hard, satiny length.

Shuddering, he folded his hand over hers again, trapping it as he tugged at her hair. "I like filthy."

"Like?" She fisted her hand around him and leaned in until she could just barely touch her tongue to the crown of his cock.

He hissed as his hips jerked, shoving between her lips before he bit off a curse and pulled back. "Fucking *hell*, sunshine."

An old nickname, ancient. He was the only person who'd ever looked at her and seen that kind of warmth, and hearing the endearment on his lips left her hungry for so much more. "Don't stop." She laid her free hand on his hip and let her fingertips bite into the hard muscle. "Show me what you want."

"I want—" He bared his teeth and hauled her up by her hair, sparking tingles along her scalp.

Then his mouth crashed into hers.

No, those sheltered fantasies couldn't compare. Noah had always been so careful with her, so she wasn't prepared for this—rough kisses and desire edged with pain. Need, the kind you didn't have a hope in hell of containing, much less controlling.

Emma whimpered as a rush of heat flooded her, left her so wet and aroused that every shifting movement sparked more heat, a never-ending cycle with Noah's mouth at the center of it.

His tongue slicked over hers, and she wrapped her arms around his neck as he hoisted her from the bed only to spill her to her back. He loomed over her, wedging his body between her legs so that the base of his cock rubbed against her pussy.

He could have slammed into her then. She was wet enough, hot enough, but he slid one hand to her hip and held her steady as he kissed her harder, rougher, *deeper.* His teeth grazed her lip and he growled, rolling his hips to slick his shaft against her clit as his tongue found hers again.

Please. She swallowed the word, along with the taste of him. She'd asked what he wanted, and this was it—she felt that in every trembling line of his body. He wanted to get her off, make her come, and then, *then* he'd fuck her.

"My pleasure," she whispered against his mouth, and arched her hips to meet his next slippery grind.

He bit her lip again, tugging at it with his teeth for a shivering heartbeat before his mouth shifted to her ear. "Is that a piercing I feel?"

It took her a second to make sense of the words, even though every flex of his hips bumped the end of the metal barbell into her clit, sending electric shocks rocketing through her. "Uh-huh," she managed. "Wanna see?"

He laughed, low and hot, and thrust against her with a slow, circular grind that left her gritting her teeth to hold back a cry. "Later. I'll get my tongue all over it."

"Tease." His eyes were so blue, deeper than the sky but not as dark as ink. She'd never seen the ocean, but maybe it was like this, like tumbling down until all you could feel was—

Holding on to his shoulders didn't give her enough leverage. She dropped her hands to the small of his back, to the swell of his ass, and swiveled her hips. Pleasure splintered through her at the directness of the contact, at the way he groaned encouragement and watched her face as if he'd never seen anything more perfect.

"Just like that," he whispered hoarsely, mirroring her movement with perfect precision. "Show me what gets you off."

Just like that. The words echoed in the buzz in her ears. His voice, rasping and hungry. *Sunshine.* Her pulse throbbed, hot and low, as she rocked her clit against his cock. *Show me.*

She never came this fast, even with her piercing. But having Noah hard against her—starving but so focused on her, rough but so fucking *careful*—drove her over the edge. The twisting tension crashed in on her, dragging a cry from her throat and curling her toes as she rode her orgasm.

He cupped her face as she stilled, his thumbs rubbing back and forth along her cheek with a gentleness that softened the harsh need in his eyes. "I want to fuck you so damn hard."

The combination of tenderness and lust undid her. *Deep. Now.* She pushed at his shoulders, lifted her body, and angled her hips until the head of his cock nudged between her pussy lips. "Take it, Noah." The strangled plea sounded far away, like it hadn't come from her lips. "Fucking take it."

One strong hand curled beneath her knee, shoving her thighs wide. "Is that what you need? Hard?"

She needed to know he was real, not some leftover remnant of childish fantasy. That he was *with her.* "I need you."

He gripped his cock, the muscles in his arms tense and trembling. He stroked the crown between her pussy lips and up, slicking it over her clit, bumping against her piercing. "How? Say it."

Emma grasped the bedspread. "Fast," she whispered,

pinned in place by his fierce gaze. "I want you to ride me, and I want it rough."

Noah positioned his cock and drove forward with one desperate thrust. He was even bigger than he looked, thick and so damn hard, pressing into her, stretching her. He didn't just fill her—he invaded her, marking her as his from the inside out. But it felt as much like submission as it did dominance, like he was giving in to the fire between them. Like he knew her pleasure was incomplete without his.

Breathtaking. She'd heard the word, used it, but never felt it as viscerally as this.

And then he was over her, hands planted on either side of her head as he thrust again, hard enough to make the sound of their hips slapping together audible in spite of his satisfied groan. "Do you have any fucking idea how good you feel?"

"No." The word spilled out on a moan as her brain scrambled to catch up with the ready heat flooding her body.

His voice lowered to a rasp as he rolled into her again, driving deep. "Do you want me to tell you? Do you like dirty words as much as you like hard fucking?"

She barely managed a pleading whimper. She didn't usually give a damn about words, dirty or not, but the way Noah wrapped his voice around every filthy syllable left her clenching in anticipation.

And that was the first word he whispered, wreathing it in fervent approval. "Clenching. Soft. Slick, because you already came all over me."

"Noah." When she lifted her legs higher, gripping his sides, the head of his cock hit her G-spot with his next thrust, and her whimpers gave way to begging. "I need it fast, please—"

He hooked one hand under her knee, forcing her calf up to his shoulder as he quickened his pace. Noah had always been smart, but now she could see the calculation in his eyes as he made minute adjustments in their positions until he was riding hard right on the spot she needed.

Her lungs burned, but oxygen had never been so unimportant. All that mattered was his dick, the unrelenting, slamming thrusts—and the way he whispered her name, almost as if he didn't even know he was doing it. As if his breath itself carried her.

That tantalizing danger lurking beneath the surface broke free. It wasn't just in his eyes anymore. His face twisted into an expression of naked hunger, jaw clenched, brow furrowed. His body loomed large above hers, muscles bunching and flexing with his unrelenting rhythm. The smiling, gentle man she'd known was gone, swept away by this dangerous stranger who fucked her like he wanted to turn her world inside-out.

Like he wanted to own her.

Emma bit back a shriek as the mounting pleasure crested, sudden and inescapable. Gripping the covers wasn't enough to keep her from spinning away, so she grabbed on to Noah. His skin burned, and it wreathed her in a satisfaction almost as visceral as the pounding, twisting bliss.

That bliss melted into a different kind of need as he groaned wordless approval. The need to show him every moment of her orgasm, to reflect it back until it took him, too.

She scratched him, her nails digging furrows into his sweat-slicked chest. "Come in me."

His pace faltered as his eyes narrowed. "Say it again."

"You heard me." She dragged her fingernails down his side, to his hipbone. "I want you to come inside me."

"Dirty," he growled before pushing upright. He pinned her in place with one hand on her thigh and splayed the other across her belly with his thumb hovering just above her clit. That was all the time she had to prepare before he slammed forward, wilder than before. No more carefully calculated thrusts chasing her pleasure. He was riding her, driving into her, chasing his own and demanding she get off on it.

He nudged her piercing, a quick flick that ricocheted through her like a shot. He held her trapped, at his mercy, and Christ, she could get addicted to this.

She couldn't get closer, and she couldn't get away, so Emma closed her eyes and let go, let him drive her higher, until the shuddering passion felt like part of her and Noah, like something that would never stop.

His fingers bit into skin as he came, a delicious slice of pain bursting through the ecstasy, and he clutched her long after his desperate rhythm stilled.

Emma lay there, frozen, as if the slightest movement could shatter the moment. She whispered his name instead, and he stretched out over her, his weight pushing her into the mattress as he caught her mouth in a lazy kiss.

She pushed at his shoulders. He rolled over, taking her with him, never breaking the kiss. So Emma finally did, resting her forehead against his with a sigh.

Noah gathered her disheveled hair with gentle fingers and swept it away from their faces. "Hey."

"Hey." A laugh bubbled up, and she let it. "Is this where things get awkward?"

His lips twitched into a half-smile. "Only if you didn't like it."

"I didn't like it." She brushed a kiss to the corner of his mouth. "I loved it. I want to do it again."

This time he laughed, running a hand down her spine to cup her ass. "Good. I made some mental notes for refining my technique."

"I bet." Emma slid to the bed beside him and propped her head on her hand. "Don't you ever get tired of think-ing?"

He turned his head to study her, his brow furrowing. "No, the thinking isn't the problem. It's never having anything good to think about."

"All the more reason to stay, isn't it?" He could ease up on his obsession with Mac Fleming, replace some of those violent thoughts with more pleasant ones. "Cib wouldn't have wanted you to live like this."

The line between his eyebrows deepened as his lips tugged into a frown. "Staying might not be as easy as you think. O'Kane wants my skills, but he may not like my baggage."

"What, your vendetta against Fleming?" Emma sat up with a snort. "I doubt it'd bother Dallas. He hates him even more than you do."

"Emma." His voice was serious, and so was his expression as he caught her arm and tugged her back down. He lifted himself on one elbow and framed her face with one hand, his thumb a firm pressure on her chin. "You need to take what I'm about to say seriously, okay? Promise me."

She tried to look away, but he wouldn't let her. "I promise."

"Mac Fleming wants me under his thumb or dead, whichever he can get." Noah closed his eyes. "I doubt he'll risk pissing off O'Kane by snatching a woman who wears his ink. That's the only reason I'm still here at all."

She, of all people, knew what a deadly bastard Mac Fleming could be. Memories she'd tried to repress bubbled up in bits and pieces—low, tense arguments, fear, the scent of blood and terrible, terrible silence. Of all the things her older brother had fought so damn hard to shield her from, the reality of life in Sector Five topped the list. The reality of Mac Fleming.

Her hand had started to shake, so she laid it on Noah's cheek. "He can't get to you here. And he doesn't know anything about you and me."

His jaw clenched under her fingers. "He could figure out that you're Cib's little sister."

She could barely think about her brother without pain, especially alongside such a harsh reminder of his bloody fate. "What does he care? Whatever problems they had died with Cib."

"He doesn't care, not about that," Noah said roughly. He opened his eyes, and they were dark again, almost blank. "But if he knows that, he'll know he can use you to get to me."

No warmth now, nothing but that flat lack of emotion. Emma shivered. "I don't know why I feel like I should apologize to you. I haven't done a damn thing wrong, except maybe exist."

"No, it's not—" He groaned and rolled away, covering his face with one hand. "It's not about me. You *haven't* done anything wrong, which is why I don't want you paying for my sins. Or Cib's."

"Then what do you want from me?"

"I want you to be safe. Happy."

And, as far as he was concerned, neither of those things could include him.

Emma reached for her robe and shrugged into it. "I'm both. You don't have to worry about me, Noah."

He moved fast, coming to his feet and catching her around the waist. Her back slammed against his chest, which felt as hard and unyielding as a brick wall as he lifted one hand to curl around her throat. "Don't do that. Don't make the mistake of calling what's inside me *worry*. Good men worry. Men like me take care of the problem."

Her breath seized in her lungs, and Emma reminded herself that Noah Lennox would never hurt her. Then again, he would never put his hand around her throat, or fuck her like he couldn't stay out of her for one more heartbeat before losing his mind.

What she knew of Noah Lennox didn't seem to be true anymore, and all bets were off.

She took a slow, deep breath. "You take care of it like you plan on taking care of Fleming?"

"Or like I took care of Clara Danforth."

Emma turned her head as far as possible, and she

could still barely see his face out of the corner of her eye. "What did you do to her?"

His breath fell hot against her cheek. "Special Tasks made her disappear tonight. She'll be lost in an Eden holding cell while they try to figure out how she managed to run a credit counterfeiting operation out of her store."

Clara was a hard woman, mercenary. She'd never had a kind word for Emma, but she'd never raised an angry hand to her, either. "Why?"

"Because she lied to me." Noah gripped her chin and tilted her head back until she could see his brutal, furious expression. "I paid for you and some bastard who probably never existed to start a new life in the mountains. You were supposed to be gone, and the whole fucking time you were right here where Fleming could have laid hands on you, could have *hurt* you, and I never would have known. Not until he wanted me to."

Emma's stomach churned. There was too much information in the words—Noah had cared enough to keep tabs on her, to watch out for her, to pay for her way out of hell. But it was the unspoken meaning lurking below it all that tore at her heart.

He said *because she lied*, but what he really meant was *because she gave me hope*.

"I'm sorry," Emma rasped. "Stealing is reason enough, but that— I'm sorry."

He shuddered. "Don't. Don't *understand*. I ruined a woman's life."

But Emma's own anger built until it spilled over into hot tears. "It's not the money. What did she do, make shit up? She lied to you, and she never once told me that you gave a damn. Not even when I left."

He spun her around with a tortured noise, dragging her into his arms with her head tucked under his chin. "I sent her money every month. For room and board, extra for art supplies. I wouldn't have left you there at all, but Fleming was after me. Fuck, he still is."

"Then it's my turn." He'd left a helpless child, a woman who couldn't protect herself. That wasn't who she was anymore. "Stay. If he comes at you, we'll show him what happens when he crosses the line with an O'Kane."

Noah exhaled, his body tense and rigid against hers. "It's more complicated than that. Fleming isn't just another thug. He could call a meeting of the sector heads and demand Dallas hand me over. And that'd be bad."

"Dallas wouldn't do it. Not only for my sake, but because he wants you here."

"Of course he does," Noah said dryly, his hands fisting on her back. "Everyone wants what I can do. But if Fleming can't have me, he'll make sure no one can."

She arched an eyebrow. "Over my dead body."

A growl rumbled through his chest and left his lips on a snarl as he forced her head back. "Don't you fucking *joke* about that."

Her eyes locked with his, and it wasn't until that moment that she realized the truth—it hadn't been a joke, not entirely. "Nothing's going to happen to me."

"No." He backed her toward the wall, letting her thump against it gently before sliding down her body. Even on his knees he looked fierce, his hands pressed to the wall on either side of her hips, strong arms penning her in place. "Nothing's going to happen to you. Not tonight, and not ever."

Her knees went weak. "You won't let it."

"No." His gaze swept up her body to burn into her. "Nothing bad. If you want something good to happen, you have to ask for it."

"Like if I want you to stay?" She nudged his side with her foot. "Not here in Sector Four. In my room, just for tonight."

"Is that all you want?" He caught her ankle and guided her foot back to the floor before letting his fingers glide up the back of her leg. "Because I was thinking about a few other ways I could show you what sort of man I am."

"What are you gonna do—throw me over the bed? Fuck me in the ass?" She shifted against the wall, rubbing her leg against his hand. "Tie me up?"

"Probably all three at once." His hand reached the back of her knee, and he folded his fingers on her inner thigh and tugged, forcing her legs apart. "But not yet. Hold yourself open for me."

"The girls in Five said you were rude as hell." She parted her pussy lips, teased the top end of the metal barbell she wore with her middle finger, and bit her lip when he growled approval and licked her fingertip.

"Emmaline Cibulski," he murmured, gazing up at her. "Were you asking them about me, or listening to the gossip?"

"I wanted to know." What he liked, what he did. Whether he'd ever do it to her.

He gripped her thigh to hold her in place and leaned closer. "What did you find out?"

Emma had to try twice just to get the words past her lips. "That you don't do anything halfway. That if a woman says yes to you, she'd better mean it. And that saying yes is worth it." As open and revealed as she was, it was easy to take it farther. All the way. "That's what the nicer girls said. The not-so-nice ones liked to make fun of me."

He made a low, angry sound that vibrated against her. "You should have told me."

The need to comfort him trumped everything else, so she slid to her knees in front of him and cupped his face. "I couldn't tell you then, and it doesn't matter now. Those things don't hurt me anymore."

Still frowning, he studied her face for a tense moment before lifting his hands to hers. "I never wanted you to hurt at all. You were always the bright spot in my world."

Four years. She'd spent four years in pain, and all because she'd never heard these words. But trusting them now—so damn wild, and so damn *fast*...

Emma shook her head. "It's late, and you're spun. You

need sleep."

He smiled again, that warm, soft smile that had been hers alone. "Still bossing me around, huh?"

Her stomach fluttered. "Someone has to take care of you."

"Is that not what I've been doing?"

She couldn't even lie, not with the image of his flat, hopeless expression so fresh in her mind. "Not just surviving, Noah. Everything else."

An amused noise escaped him, something torn between a snort and a laugh. "You know how crazy that sounds? In most of the other sectors, survival's as good as it gets. Hard to imagine something more."

Her own lips tugged up in response, so the kiss she brushed over the corner of his mouth was more like a smile. "Welcome to Sector Four."

3

H E KNEW IT was a nightmare, because he'd relived it a hundred times.

That didn't make it any easier to wake up.

Cib's hands were shaking. Noah watched him try to light his cigarette, the flame always jerking away from the tip at the last second. He finally managed it, then sat back to run those same trembling fingers through his dark, spiky hair. "Matty says Fleming's got extra shipments this month. Sector runs."

"Fuck, Cib. Sector runs are dangerous." The words tumbled out of his mouth—not the ones he'd said that night, but close enough. He'd muttered a hundred varia-tions, and it always ended the same way.

Wake up, Lennox. Wake up.

"But they pay." Cib hopped off the crate and started to pace the width of the alley, kicking trash out of his path. "I need something big, man, or I'm never gonna get my sister out of this shithole."

"I told you I'm working on it. That place in the mountains will take all of us, but they need goods or cash up front—"

But Cib wasn't listening. He never did. "Gotta settle some debts, too. Nothing bad."

It was a lie. There were always more debts than Cib admitted to, big ones that explained his nervous energy and bloodshot eyes. Noah hadn't seen it then, hadn't *wanted* to see it. He'd needed to believe his friend was too smart to snort Mac Fleming's needlessly addictive products up his nose.

Noah didn't ask the question that had come next, but it wouldn't be his worst nightmare if that could make a damn bit of difference.

"The, uh—" Cib licked his cracked lips. "Last week's deliveries here in Five hit a snag. Me and Klein, we got—" He laughed, forced and fake. "We got rolled by a couple of assholes. They took it all, the money and the drugs. Everything we were holding for Fleming."

More bullshit. Transparent bullshit, lies Noah *hadn't* been able to ignore, because if anyone had stolen Fleming's drugs within the boundaries of Sector Five, he would have sent his chief enforcer to tear the sector apart—and tear the sorry bastard's arms from his body.

"How much, Cib?"

Instead of a number, an *answer*, his best friend muttered the words that spun the scene down deeper into terror. "You know, uh, I've been thinking. And I had this sort of idea..."

Panic gripped Noah, the sick dread of what was coming, and even in a hazy fucking dream he knew it would be worse this time. Worse because something had happened, something had changed—

"Emmy likes you." Cib wouldn't look at him, but he wouldn't stop, either. "She really, really likes you, man."

Wake up. Wake the fuck up. Goddamn *it.*

"Hell." Cib laughed again, shrill and damning. "I think she might lov—"

The street shattered around him, falling away as Noah lunged out of bed, his panting breaths too loud in the darkness. A sharp moment of disorientation vanished when Emma murmured a muffled protest behind him.

He tensed, waiting for any sound to indicate she'd woken up, but her breathing settled back into an even rhythm, and he scrubbed his hands over his face as if that would erase the lingering horror.

At least he'd woken up before the real nightmare kicked in. Cib's voice, shaking with desperation and a starving edge that couldn't have really existed, because surely Noah would have noticed. Guilt played with the memory, adding a hundred clues he should have caught, torturing him with his failure night after fucking night.

He swept up his pants and shirt by feel and pulled them on as his eyes adjusted to the thin light coming from beneath the door. Emma had twisted in her sleep, twining the sheets around one calf and leaving most of her naked body bare. Her tattoos were indistinct shadows weaving intriguing patterns over her skin, unfamiliar enough to shake him out of the past.

She wasn't the same girl she'd been, and he still didn't know if that was a good thing. He could have scared the old Emma off with a little roughness or some dirty talk. This one had taken both in stride before promising to protect him.

Of course, if he really wanted to get rid of her, all he had to do was tell her the truth about how his nightmare ended.

Shuddering, Noah grabbed his boots and slipped into the hallway. It was early—too early for a bunch of people who drank and fucked into the wee hours of the morning, apparently—but he'd barely gotten his laces tied when the redhead he'd seen tending bar the previous night turned the corner.

Something about her features nagged at him, a familiarity he couldn't quite place. Odd, because she wasn't the
kind of woman a man forgot—tall and built, with killer
curves she dressed to full advantage.

She slowed to a stop before smiling. "You sneaking
out, Noah?"

It wasn't a stretch to imagine that the O'Kanes knew
who he was, but something about the teasing edge to the
words brought that familiarity crashing in on him, and he
was suddenly *sure* he'd heard her say his name before,
with that same husky laughter beneath it.

No, not laughter. The last time that voice had spoken
his name, it had trembled with the disconnected dreami-
ness of someone stoned out of her mind.

He snapped his gaze back to her face and imagined
her leaner, paler. Her cheekbones stark beneath sunken
eyes, all those healthy curves gone. "Tracy?"

"In the flesh." She rested a hand on her hip and tilted
her head. "A little more of it these days. How are you?"

"Surprised. You were pretty...stuck." A nice word for
how he'd last seen her, shaking for a hit, willing to do
damn near anything to get one. Only one thing had kept
her out of the brothels, off the streets, separated her from
a hundred other junkies—special treatment from Fleming's chief enforcer.

Finn hadn't bothered with rules or explanations, not
where Tracy was concerned. She got her drugs from him,
full stop. Anyone who tried to trade her flesh for a fix lost
whatever body part they'd laid on her. The only moron
dumb enough to try it twice had disappeared.

Some of the really strung-out girls had called it romantic. For Noah, it had been a cautionary tale, one
ground deeper into his psyche every time Tracy crawled
out of Finn's lap, flying high and oblivious to the self-
loathing in the man's eyes.

"Stuck," she echoed softly. "That's one way to put it.
Not anymore, though." She looked away. "You and Emma

working things out?"

"Tracy—"

"It's Trix now."

He couldn't help but raise an eyebrow at the nick-name. "Trix."

"Hey, truth in advertising, right?" She nodded past him, to Emma's door. "She's asked me some things. About stuff I guess you didn't tell her."

Jesus Christ. Tracy—*Trix*—had lived at ground zero, in the sick, rotting heart of Fleming's empire. Tucked into Finn's pocket, she could have heard anything. *Everything.* "How much does she know about what her brother did?"

"Some about the drugs." Trix caught his eye with a pointed look. "Nothing about the money."

"Good." It came out too forceful, and he modulated his tone. "She doesn't need to know, all right? Anything Cib might have done or said—that was the drugs, not her brother. There's no damn reason to take him away from her."

"I wouldn't," Trix retorted. "But she'll find out eventu-ally. Neither of us can stop that, not unless you plan on razing Sector Five."

"Not entirely."

Understanding washed over her face. "So *that's* why you're here. I thought—" She shook her head. "Never mind."

He could see the truth in her eyes. She'd thought he'd come back for Emma, because she'd known him before he'd locked away emotion and affection out of necessity. "Did everyone know?"

Trix stared at him for a long, hard second, then shrugged wearily. "Emma didn't."

It was a struggle not to grind his teeth. "I'm more wor-ried about people who might hurt her to get to me. If they figure it out..."

"They'll know where to hit you," she agreed with a nod. "People around here wouldn't say anything. She's wearing O'Kane ink now."

He wanted to believe it was that simple, but O'Kane and Fleming represented two sides of the same criminal coin. They peddled their respective vices with such dedication that people had dubbed the wide road separating their sectors Sin Street. Brothels and gambling houses of varying classes lined both sides, with the road marking the invisible line between booze and drugs.

Both were quick paths to oblivion, and both destroyed lives. But Fleming turned his hand to legitimate business, too, producing medications essential to a comfortable life in Eden. He should have been the one with the power and the influence, not a glorified bootlegger with a reputation for being too distracted by his dick to care about politics.

Noah studied Trix's face again. "You've seen both sides. Is she safe here?"

The woman's matter-of-fact expression softened into sympathy. "Mac Fleming is scared shitless of Dallas O'Kane. That's as safe as it gets out here in the sectors, wouldn't you say?"

That depended on why he was so damn scary—but the pride in Trix's eyes said enough. Plenty of men in Five obeyed Fleming out of fear or greed or desperation, but precious few looked at him with any sort of fondness.

If O'Kane's men were half as loyal to him as the women seemed to be, he had himself a tidy little army that would do more than kill for him. They'd die for him, or maybe even for each other.

Maybe even for Emma.

"Yeah," he said, ignoring the hollow ache in his chest. It should have been a weight off his shoulders, one less thing holding him back from achieving his goal. "It sounds pretty damn safe."

"Doesn't mean she doesn't need you," Trix said softly.

Living underground away from people had made him fucking careless with his feelings. Noah hardened his expression and forced a shrug. "It'd be better for her if she didn't. Like you said. The truth always comes out."

"Yeah." She glanced down the hall. "You cutting out?"

He deserved the judgment in her voice. It was damn tempting to pick up and *run*, past the boundaries of the sectors, past the communes where people toiled to provide bread for Eden's fancy tables. There were places out there. The mountain communities, other cities. The world had ground to a halt, but people kept going. They always kept going.

If he cared at all for Emma, he'd do it. Make this a clean cut, instead of coming back to dig under her skin, just so he could steal a few more memories before she learned enough to drive him away. "I need a few things from Three, some tech and a couple changes of clothes. I'll be back."

Trix hummed and continued her walk down the hall. "I'll see you then."

Hard to say if she believed him, but shit, he didn't even know if he believed himself. After a shower and a change of clothes, he wouldn't be able to smell Emma on his skin anymore, and maybe that would give him the strength to do the right thing.

Or maybe it would only leave him crazy at the loss, and that much more determined to come back and lose himself in her all over again.

When Emma woke up, Noah was gone.

She stared at the empty, rumpled spot on her bed for what seemed like forever, her mind spinning in a million different directions, always coming back to the same gut-clenching fact.

He'd never said he would stay past the night.

Finally, she dragged herself out of bed and hit the shower. Standing under the steaming spray did little to ease the ache in her chest, but at least it cleared her head.

He'd left her before, and she'd handled it. She wasn't a child anymore, nineteen years old and huddled at the back door of Clara's shop, fighting tears as she watched Noah melt into the night.

By the time she climbed out to dry her hair and put on her makeup, she'd almost convinced herself it didn't matter. No promises meant no promises broken. That was Noah's style.

Emma was an O'Kane. They'd all survived worse.

She stopped for coffee on the way to the studio, because Christ knew Ace would need it. Sure enough, he'd slept there again, on the beat-up couch nestled against the far wall, behind the workspace. Silly, since it wasn't long enough for someone of his height, and his legs hung over the end.

Normally, Emma would have reminded him that he had a perfectly serviceable bed somewhere, possibly even joked about whether it was filled over capacity again. Not today, not after her own amazing night—and equally shitty morning.

She shoved a mug of coffee at him instead.

Ace accepted it and swung his feet to the floor, somehow managing to roll into a seated position without spilling the steaming drink all over his bare chest. "Jesus, kid. You're up early."

"It's almost eleven," she retorted, slinging her bag over her head.

"Yeah, like I said. Early."

Emma avoided his gaze. "I have some stuff to work on."

"Uh-huh." Ace sipped the coffee before slapping a hand on the couch cushion next to him. "Or you could park your ass and tell me what's up with that stone-faced nerd you were grinding up on last night. Why so glum, junior? Did he have a tiny dick?"

"Jesus, no." She dropped beside him and pushed her hair out of her face. "That wasn't a nerd. It was Noah."

"I know it was—" Ace stopped and tilted his head. "Wait, Lennox is *the* Noah? The one who got you out of Five?"

The words elicited another shudder of unwanted memory. Her brother's pale, broken face. Noah's voice, begging her to calm down and tell him what she'd seen.

Running.

Emma shook herself. "Noah was my brother's best friend."

Ace set his mug on the floor and wrapped an arm around her, tugging her against the warm, solid bulk of his body. "So he came back. Took him fucking long enough."

"He didn't come back for me." The words hung in her throat, metal shards that scraped and cut. "He's planning on taking Fleming down, and he needs Dallas's help for that."

"Well, that makes him delusional on top of stupid." Ace caught her chin and tipped her head back. "Say the word, junior, and I'll have Cruz break him into as many pieces as you want. No one fucks with my apprentice."

"I don't want him broken." Though Christ knew Ace would do it anyway when she admitted the truth. "He left this morning before I woke up. I don't know if he'll be back, or if he's gone for good, or *what*."

Ace's chest rumbled in an irritated growl. "Forget Cruz. He'll be too efficient."

"Work," Emma said firmly. "When are you gonna let me design something for you?"

"Oh, is *that* how it is?" Ace's lips twitched as he released her. "Someone just wants to get her hands on my beautiful skin."

A chance to save her pride, if nothing else. She blinked up at him and smiled. "You promised."

"Uh-huh." He slapped her hip and urged her off the couch. "Grab your sketchpad. If it'll cheer you up, I'll let you violate the temple of my body."

She snagged a pad from the drawing desk closest to the couch. "Black-and-gray or color?"

Sometimes he made her design black-and-gray tattoos over and over again, just because he knew it wasn't her preference, but today he grinned at her. "Your choice. Sky's the limit, kid. I want to see the best you've got."

She arched an eyebrow as she gathered her colored pens. "No guidelines?"

"None." He rolled to his feet and turned. "Anything that'll fit along my spine."

Her momentary optimism dissolved with a groan. Ace's back was bare for a reason—he never liked a damn thing he or anyone else dreamed up to put on it. "Fool's errand. I get it."

Ace cast her an unsympathetic look over his shoulder. "Don't whine, kid. I knew the first time I saw one of your drawings that you were gonna be the one. So stop pulling your punches and make some fucking art."

Kid. She held up her middle finger, but he'd already disappeared into the back, so she dropped to the desk and uncapped a pen. She was still staring at the paper when the shower in the washroom cut on.

She sketched a heart—not a basic, flat one, but a three-dimensional, stylized shape.

Kid.

Maybe Noah was hung up on the same thing, as if the four years that had passed didn't exist, and she was the same poor girl from Sector Five, the one with a dead brother and bleak prospects. The one who'd probably wind up in Fleming's stable of whores—if she was lucky.

Maybe he regretted their night together, and that was why he'd crept out without waking her.

Her pen accidentally scratched across the paper, and she worked the mark into her design, turning it into a thread of barbed wire. It wrapped around the heart, points almost but not quite piercing to draw blood—

And suddenly she knew exactly what she was going to

design for Ace. Stop pulling her punches, he'd said. *Make some fucking art.*

She reached for the other pens and fleshed out the design, then began to color it in, and she was just finishing up one last swoop of gold when Ace braced a hand on the table beside her and leaned over her shoulder.

He stared for long enough to kindle fluttering nerves in her stomach, and she prepared herself for the one word she'd gotten every previous time, always delivered in the same easy, friendly tone of dismissal. *Nope.*

Ace straightened. "Better."

Her heart skipped a beat, and she capped her pen. "But not great."

"Technically, it's solid." He traced a finger along the edge of the paper. "A little on the nose. Make them ask the question, don't give them the answer."

A warning lurked just under his admonition—people wanted truth, but only so much of it. "Understood. But I'm gunning for your job, Santana. I won't be designing flash forever."

"No shit, you won't." Ace squeezed her shoulder. "You remember that if your nerd comes crawling back. Give me another couple years, and you'll be able to barter your skills for any goddamn thing you want. Ink talks in Sector Four, and you're gonna be one of the best."

Emma had to swallow past the lump in her throat, and she covered his hand with hers. "Thanks, Ace."

"Aww, don't go getting mushy on me." He leaned past her and ripped the page out of her sketchbook, leaving her with a fresh one. "Give me a nice bloody heart and dagger this time. One of the fighters is coming in this afternoon, and if he likes what you come up with, you can do his tattoo."

"Yeah?"

Ace grinned as he folded her drawing and tucked it into his pocket. "You're already better than all the stencil-tracing posers in the marketplace combined. If you weren't, you wouldn't be my apprentice."

A challenge, and the perfect thing to distract her from thoughts of Noah. Either he'd show up again or he wouldn't, but either way, one thing could never change.

She was an O'Kane, and her family would always have her back.

4

BEFORE HE'D TAKEN two steps into the tattoo studio, Noah knew Emma had found her home.

The abstract knowledge had been there, but his gut must have still believed there was some future where they ran off to the mountains and lived out the imaginary life he'd bought for her all those years ago. It was the only explanation for the *loss* that hit him, like a truck careening out of control.

The woman on the stage, flashing knives as she stripped—that was a stranger. So was the woman who'd climbed into his lap and goaded him into the hottest sex he'd ever had, the one who'd listened to his filthy words and sworn to protect him. A beautiful, hauntingly familiar stranger, but the Emma he'd known hadn't *fit* in any of those situations.

She fit here. The studio was surprisingly large, with plenty of space around the tattoo chair situated in the center. It was book-ended by a table and a few rolling trays covered with a familiar array of instruments, but that wasn't what struck him. It was the artwork lining all four walls, a joyous jumble of pre-Flare masterpieces in gilded frames and hasty sketches taped over one another.

And in between the artwork—shelf upon shelf of supplies. Markers. Pens. Paints. Charcoal and pencils and stacks of sketchpads and thick, creamy paper, the kind they manufactured in Sector Eight and mostly sold to Eden. You could buy a kidney cheaper than you could the contents of just one of these shelves, and there had to be two dozen.

Emma was sketching at one of the tables set against the wall, her hair twisted up from her neck and her arms bare, a sight so familiar his heart lurched. She always changed into a tank top before settling in to draw, claiming she didn't like working in sleeves.

Even Cib had never dreamed of being able to give her this. And as selfish as Noah was for coming back at all, he wasn't enough of a bastard to try to take her away from it.

She didn't look up until she finished one curving line, her wrist twisting in a delicate arc. Her eyes locked with his, dark and guarded, and she laid down her pen. "Hi."

"Hey." And just like that the familiarity was gone, because the Emma who'd complained about long-sleeved shirts getting in her way had never looked at him with eyes this wary. "Noelle said I'd find you here."

"It's usually a safe bet." Emma rose, and her stool skittered a few feet across the floor. "I thought you'd left."

There was no apology or excuse that justified sneaking out of her room without so much as a note, not when he hadn't been sure if he was coming back. "I didn't."

Her lips twisted in a half-smile. "I guess."

Not enough. He shoved his hands into his jacket pockets to hide the fact he'd curled them into fists. "I'm sorry. I shouldn't have cut out like that."

"No, you shouldn't have." Emma propped her hands on

her hips and faced him squarely. "I deserved better than that. Especially after—" The words cut off abruptly.

He could blame the nightmare, but he'd have to open a box he wanted safely shut for as long as possible. So he took the hit square on the chin and made himself feel the pain. He deserved it. "It wasn't about you," he lied. "I left some shit in Three that I didn't want unguarded for long. Just in case."

"Okay." She rocked back on her heels and nodded toward the couch along the back wall. "You want to sit?"

It was a reprieve, if not forgiveness, but he snatched at it. "Can I see what you're working on?"

Instead of showing him, she picked up the sketchbook and held it close to her chest. "It's nothing. I was just fucking around with a design from earlier. Ace says it still needs work."

Ace. Plenty of the O'Kanes had files, but none as lurid as Alexander Santana's. In Eden, he was best known for a series of paintings he'd done almost a decade ago, paintings rumored to have been gifts to the rich women he'd slept with in exchange for their patronage.

Ownership of a Santana had led to divorce and scandal more than once, which only added to their legend and increased their value among a certain set.

Noah had seen enough pictures of the paintings in question to know the man had skill. It was one more thing he and Cib had never been able to supply—a teacher.

Squashing jealousy, Noah tried for a smile. It stretched his mouth in unfamiliar ways, but maybe it was the kind of habit that muscle memory could restore. "C'mon, Em. Just a peek?"

She looked like she was going to say no, but then she flipped the sketchbook around and held it out for him to see.

She'd drawn a heart with a keyhole at its center, effortlessly shaded to make it three dimensional. Barbed wire and chains crisscrossed each other around it, so intricately sketched that he could make out the individual twists of wire and the sharp, pointed tips of the barbs. "It's a tattoo?"

"It is." She wiggled the pad of paper. "You want this one? It suits you."

More than she'd ever know. "It's not meant for some-one else?"

The notebook hit the desk with a soft thump, and Emma turned away. "I was kidding."

"No, you're right." He shrugged out of his jacket and stripped his shirt over his head. "If I'm going to hang around the O'Kane compound, I should have at least one tattoo, right?"

She sucked in a breath. For a moment, her gaze lin-gered on his chest, soft with memory. Then her eyes shuttered, and she folded her arms across her body, one hip cocked out in a pose that screamed challenge. "I'm not that easy. You want ink? You have to pay."

Good for you. "All right. Cash, credits, or infor-mation?"

"Information," she said immediately. "Answers."

Of course. The one thing only he could give her, and the quickest path back out of her life. But he liked her like this—tough, challenging. Unafraid to demand what she wanted. "Just as long as you know I'm not easy, either. Anything that could put you in danger's gonna cost more than a tattoo."

"Fair enough." She gestured to the antique tattoo chair. "Have a seat."

Noah tossed his shirt over the table and sank into the chair. "How do other people pay for tattoos?"

"Depends." Tiny plastic cups rattled on one of the trays as she laid them out, side by side. "O'Kanes get certain ones for free, obviously. More if Ace is feeling generous. Someone off the street better bring cash, clean credits, or damn good favors. He barters sometimes, too."

"Did he do yours?"

Emma grinned as she dropped to another rolling stool and pulled the tray to rest beside the tattoo chair. "Ace would have a hissy if I let anyone else do my ink. He gave me my first one a few years back—I'd heard he was the best, so I saved up and brought him one of my designs. Been in and out of this shop ever since."

He quirked an eyebrow. "Are you adding my questions to my bill?"

Her grin gentled into a smile. "Maybe." She pressed the design notebook face down against a thinner sheet of paper, then ran them both quickly under a light fixed to the bottom of the rolling tray. The image appeared on the thin sheet, and she held up the paper. "Where do you want it?"

"Wherever you think is best." This was fascinating, too. Watching her so sure and confident, totally in her element. She looked the way he felt surrounded by terminal screens—in control.

She considered him for a moment, then cleaned a spot on the left side of his chest. "Here, I think." When she pressed the light-processed paper to his wet skin and lifted it once more, it left a blue image of the design behind. "Perfect."

Right over his own frozen heart. "Yeah."

He watched in silence as she slipped on a pair of gloves and reached for a tube of gel. He couldn't read the label, but Fleming's pharmaceutical logo was plastered across the side, something that Noah might have brooded over if Emma wasn't about to put her hands all over him.

The gel was cold, but it warmed against his skin as she smoothed it over the transferred design. "First question," she whispered.

He didn't let himself tense. "Okay."

"What did you go get this morning from Sector Three?" Her gaze flicked up to lock with his. "I'm assuming you only went to Three."

"Yeah." Not a tough question, and one he could answer

honestly. "I needed some clothes and some tech. And I wanted to set a couple traps in case I'm gone for a while. I can't afford to have anyone get into my place."

"Will you show it to me sometime?"

He hesitated. Most people thought he lived in some dank cave or retrofitted basement, some gloomy underground lair, scraping by and making do. The truth was far more dangerous, a family secret that could lead to Eden bombing more than one sector off the map.

And yet.

Emma, in his domain. A place he fit as cleanly as she did here, a place where *he* was in control. If he'd known for sure four years ago that the bunker was more than family legend, he would have disappeared into the tunnels beneath Three with her to start with. But it had taken him seven months to find it, and by then...

By then, she'd almost been gone.

"Is that a no?" She changed her gloves, plucked up a bottle of black ink, and poured a little into one of the tiny cups she'd set out.

"No, it's..." They were alone in the studio, but he still lowered his voice. "It's a dangerous secret to know, for reasons I can't even explain without showing you. So make sure you really want to know first."

"Mmm." Emma tilted her head and filled the rest of the ink cups, then began to put together her machine. "Second question. How'd you like the party last night?"

"What, the orgy?" His lips tugged up, and he struggled to school his expression. "I was a little too distracted to appreciate it properly. This girl I used to know was touching herself right in front of me."

"Oh, is that all I am to you?" she teased, and the machine cut on with a menacing buzz. "A girl you used to know?"

Christ, the warmth in the words heated his blood. He welcomed the sting of the needles at this point, though he doubted something as mundane as pain would get his dick under control. "Is that your next question?"

"Nope." She slid closer and laid her free hand on his shoulder. "I know better."

Her face was close to his, her gaze intent on his chest. He could look his fill, memorize the shape of her brow and the set of her lips when she was concentrating. He could answer her question anyway, see what expression flashed through those eyes. "You were never just a girl I knew."

Her throat worked as she swallowed, but she didn't look at him. "What was I?"

"Exactly what I told you last night. The bright spot in my world."

She released a long, slow breath. "Right." But she shook it off by the time the needle touched his skin, jabbing into him with a hollow ache, and her smile was back in place. "Favorite color?"

She was retreating. Scrambling away from dangerous territory, and it should have been a relief. But he liked the challenge better, the thrill of walking the tightrope.

Or maybe he was just another asshole guy drunk on the chase, because he dropped his voice to the lowest, most suggestive fucking whisper he could manage. "Pink."

Emma didn't blush, and she didn't stammer out an embarrassed deflection. She met his gaze with a soft laugh and an arched eyebrow. "Yeah? I'm kind of fond of it myself."

Christ, that was hot. "So when Noelle said the two of you were close, she was talking biblically?"

"She gets a little adventurous now and then. I'm happy to oblige."

Noah fell silent, lost for a moment in that visual. Maybe that was the method to Dallas O'Kane's madness, the only way to reconcile his mercenary reputation with the contented loyalty of his people—even the women.

No, especially the women, because that was what was different here. Emma could be anything she wanted, *do* anything—or anyone—she wanted, and her happiness was part of the puzzle. The women here were woven in with the men, stronger and better for it.

Mac Fleming had a wife and a string of mistresses. Dallas O'Kane had a partner.

"Did you do them, too?"

Noah blinked and glanced at Emma. "What?"

"The drugs. It's my next question." She pressed her lips together as she dipped her needle into the ink again. "Were you into the same shit my brother was all fucked up on?"

A swift kick in the balls couldn't have brought him down faster. "No. I did some—the nonaddictive stuff that keeps you alert and focused. But I never got into the recreational drugs, and I wouldn't have gone near the shit Fleming cooks up to hook people. I didn't know Cib had, not until it was too damn late."

"Okay."

Her face was an impassive mask, and the persistent prick of the needles felt like a punishment now, a well-earned one. "I should have kept a closer eye on him. For all I know, it was my fault."

The corner of her mouth curved up in a mirthless smile as she shook her head. "Is that what you tell yourself? That you could have stopped him?"

"Wouldn't you?"

"You're assuming I didn't try," she answered flatly. "That I didn't *beg* him to give it up before it all went too far."

Belatedly, Noah realized what he'd said and gripped the chair to keep from jerking upright. "I didn't mean—Fuck, Emma. You were barely more than a kid. And I'm the reason he got into that world to begin with. It *was* my fault."

"Cut it out." Her tone was still flat, but firm this time. Steely. "I'm not into the blame shit. It's past, it's over. Cib made his choices. It's just..." She shrugged. "I guess by the time he regretted them, he couldn't find his way back."

"Blame Fleming," Noah told her roughly. "Nothing he sells has to be addictive. He made *that* choice, and that's why I want to bring him down."

"Works for me." She shut off the machine and started unscrewing the metal tip that held the needle. "You need to take a break before I start in again?"

He'd barely felt the pain. Even now it was more sore than anything else, like gently abraded skin. He'd gotten far worse scraping his arm on concrete. "Nah, it's fine."

"No more questions," she offered. "You're paid up."

It had been too easy, and nothing about life in the sectors was ever easy. Emma focused on her work, handling the machine and its complicated parts with long familiarity, leaving Noah crawling back over the answers he'd given her.

No, the words he'd given her. He knew better than most that words were merely the outer layer, the most basic syntax of communication. Only Emma knew what truths she'd read into what he said and how he said it, and he supposed that whatever she'd gotten had satisfied her.

Whether that was good or bad... Fuck, he was already a mile past knowing, because he'd had a darker reason for cutting out without a warning, a reason so selfish and self-absorbed he could barely admit it to himself. The answer to a question he had no right to even ask.

Now he knew Emma could forgive him.

5

D ALLAS'S GIRLFRIEND MADE Noah nervous.

Alexa Parrino—Lex, to the people in Sector Four— might not appreciate being referred to as someone's girlfriend, but Noah didn't think she'd begrudge him the nerves. A woman with her training could put a man at ease if she wanted to.

And Lex clearly didn't want to.

She stared at him from across the desk, tapping her pen on its smooth surface. "Did you have a nice trip home, Lennox?"

"I got in and out in one piece."

"So I see." She gave him an appraising look, then shrugged. "You're not a prisoner here. You can do whatever you want. But we can't guarantee your safety off this compound, and especially not outside this sector."

Noah raised an eyebrow. "I figured you'd be more concerned with the danger that might follow me back."

"See, and I figured you'd be smart enough to handle all the worrying on that count. For Emma's sake, if nothing else."

He'd walked right into that trap, and judging by the knowing glint in Lex's gaze, his nervousness had been justified. The words hadn't even been a question—she'd stated the truth like she knew it.

She probably did. "Trix talked to you."

"I talked to Trix," she corrected. "There's a difference."

"Is there?"

"Yeah, because I asked. She didn't volunteer. Though I guess that only matters if you care who's keeping your secrets." Lex braced her elbows on the desk. "But then, you seem like a man who prizes his secrets."

His heart slammed against his rib cage, a painful jolt that had him gripping the arms of the chair. "I don't know what she told you, but some truths—" He forced himself to take a slow, calming breath. "Emma has a dead brother who loved her. I'm not taking that away."

Lex shot across the desk and wound her hand in the front of Noah's shirt. "Now, you listen to me. If you tell her the truth, I will *kick your ass* so hard you won't have to walk back to Three. You'll land there."

Disengaging himself from her grip would involve touching her, and Noah wasn't sure Dallas O'Kane would let him keep his hands if he tried. Besides, he was too busy choking on relief—intense, dizzy *gratitude*. "Do I look like I want to tell her?"

"Guilt does funny things to a man. Starts eating you from the inside out, and one night you get a little drunk and figure unburdening your soul's the way to go." She released him and straightened, glaring down at him with fire in her eyes. "Emma's a nice girl. She deserves the truth, but it's got to happen the right way. If you hurt her trying to make yourself feel better, you'll regret it."

"I will," Noah agreed, quiet and easy. "If I hurt her for any reason, I'll regret it, which is why staying here is dangerous. Secrets have a way of coming out when too many people know them—and a lot of people in Five know this one."

Some of Lex's anger melted, and she sighed roughly as she stepped back. "Do you want to stay?"

Before yesterday, *no* would have come easily and honestly. "That's irrelevant."

"Why?"

"Because other priorities take precedence. *Emma* takes precedence."

Was that a flash of sympathy in her eyes? "She's not your responsibility anymore."

Because she was an O'Kane now. Because this woman owned her people as surely as any queen, and would guard the duty of protecting them as closely as she did their loyalty. It was a different kind of relief, having that confirmed. Bittersweet, because he'd had the opportunity to be the one who kept Emma safe, and he'd screwed it up.

But he couldn't let go. "I'll always be responsible for her. I may just have to reconsider the best way of keeping her safe."

"She's as safe as she can get." Lex pulled a cigarette out of a silver case and lit it. "If you're going to go, it needs to be soon. You know that, right?"

"I know." Noah leaned forward, bracing his elbows on his knees, and reminded himself that this was for Emma. "The stronger you are, the more secure she is. So tell me why O'Kane's so hot to recruit me, and I'll make it happen before I leave."

"You're supposed to be a genius, Lennox. You know why." For the first time, Lex smiled down at him. "Information and services. Information, you can give us from anywhere. But Dallas has something he'd like for you to work on here, too. A program."

Since he'd yet to see a scrap of tech more advanced than Emma's tattoo machine, he raised an eyebrow. "A program, huh?"

"Yeah." She pulled a key out of a drawer and slid it across the desk to fall into his hand. "Time to see if you're half as good as your reputation, hacker."

Watching Noah work was an old habit Emma could definitely fall back into.

"This is unreal." He crouched in front of one of the shelves and tugged out a box labeled in Noelle's meticulous cursive as *Miscellaneous: Surveillance Related.* "You could build any goddamn thing out of the parts he's got here."

"Dallas never throws anything away." She knelt beside him and peered into the box. "That's the stuff Rachel pulled off a downed Eden drone last year."

"Might be able to put a functional one back together with it, too." He pushed the box back into place and looked in the next one. "Lots of memory chips, that's good. Those are hard to get these days."

The tone of his voice—distracted but still intense— brought back a rush of memories, and she bit her lip against a smile. "Noelle put something together for you."

He rose and followed her to the table, where a workstation had been constructed with a slim keyboard resting in front of one of the biggest tablet screens they had—the kind Nessa and Noelle liked to play movies on.

Noah spun the chair around and straddled it before swiping his fingers across the screen. It sparked to life, bathing his face in harsh white light as he narrowed his eyes.

His gaze flicked back and forth for a quiet minute, and he frowned. "Huh. Edwin Cunningham's daughter did this?"

Emma punched him on the arm. "She's smart. And she says she doesn't know much, but you're the only other person I've ever met who could handle this kind of tech."

"Hey, no arguments here." He nudged her in the side with his elbow. "But there's no fucking way someone in Eden taught a councilman's daughter how to code like this. She must be like you. Naturally gifted."

Emma's cheeks heated. The praise wasn't new, but there was something different about hearing it now that their circumstances had changed so much. "Thanks."

"It's the truth." He swiped his fingers across the screen, rearranging windows full of code with half his attention. "My father had me learning how to do this before I was five years old. And I'm good, but it was never like you are with the art. You just *do it.*"

"Uh-huh." She leaned over him. This close, she could smell soap, leather, and a hint of mint, of all things. "Did Lex tell you anything about Noelle's program?"

"Nope. I think she's testing me." A furrow formed between his brows. "But from what it looks like... Oh, shit."

When he started laughing, Emma knew he'd figured it out. "Uh-huh. It's like that."

"Naughty girl, spying on Eden," Noah said, still grinning. "And tricky, but I can see where she's gotten tripped up. She's dumping all the data from the access points broadcasting past Eden's walls, but I bet she didn't realize just how far out some of the signals go. No one does."

A system monitoring all the data traffic in and out of Eden was one thing, but what he was talking about was something entirely different. "How far do they go?"

"Farther than even Eden knows." A swipe of his hand cleared the tablet, and he pulled up a program he'd showed her before, a digital art application where you drew directly on the screen. She'd never liked it—how could you feel your art when you couldn't *feel* it?—but she watched silently as he used it for a more practical purpose.

"This is the city," he said, drawing a circle with his finger. He drew the four spokes coming out of it in the cardinal directions next, and then the diagonals, dividing the outside into eight sections. "And the sectors. In the original designs, there was supposed to be a secondary wall." He drew a larger circle to encompass all of it. "That wasn't finished before the solar flares, but they'd already laid the groundwork. The tunnels, wires for power and networking. Everything but the wall itself, basically."

Emma stared at the screen. "So Eden isn't self-contained at all. The sectors are wired for access to their systems."

"Yup. The only way for Eden to be truly off-the-grid was to make sure all the support structures were connected. This was all in the original plans, but..." He trailed off and slanted a look at her. "How much do you know about what happened when the grid went down?"

Only the secondhand stories she'd heard curled up at her grandmother's knee—the darkness of the big blackout, followed by the almost magical appearance of the aurora borealis, all shades of green and blue and red, extending much farther to the south than it should have. "I know a solar storm knocked out the power grid. Destroyed it. The Flare."

Noah snorted. "They should have called it the Surge, because that's where things really went wrong. There was a technical failure in the systems that were supposed to prevent a power surge from wiping data, and it cascaded. Every device connected to the network fried, and it was anarchy."

"And the lights went out." It should have been more horrifying, to think of an innocent, comfortable world, gone in an instant. But Emma felt simple wonder that there ever could have been a society that knew only light and ease.

"Except in Eden, because it wasn't online yet. Nothing to fry." Noah circled his finger around the wall again, drawing in a second, overlapping line. "My grandfather was one of the founders, you know. It was supposed to be some big dream, the first high-tech green city. Totally self-contained, totally sustainable. They were going to prove it was possible."

Instead, it had become a prison, a place where citizens' thoughts and feelings were policed as much as their actions. "What happened?"

"Good people had something valuable, so bad people took it from them."

"Men with smaller ideas—and bigger guns?"

"Smart girl." Noah swiped his hand across the screen, banishing the drawing. "They killed my grandfather."

His hands were busy, so she squeezed his arm. "I'm sorry."

He shrugged. "He died five years before I was born. All I ever knew about him were the stories, and my father... Well, you know how my father was."

Emma remembered the man's eyes—red-rimmed and bloodshot, a dull version of Noah's bright blue. "He was pretty fried by the time I met him." It was hard to imagine he'd once been one of the best hackers in the sectors.

"I guess he was." He rearranged the windows on the screen again before pulling the keyboard closer. "The drugs made him dumb, but they didn't make him mean. He was that way from the start, bitter and angry. That's why he hacked Eden's files while everything was still in chaos. There's no record now of the outer access points and control rooms having ever existed."

"So they're there, but Eden doesn't know about them?"

"Emmy..." His fingers hovered over the keyboard, and he glanced at her. "What I've already told you is dangerous. You get that, right? I'm not even talking about Fleming now. You could disappear into a holding cell in Eden and never come out."

Her heart pounded against her breastbone. Her entire life had been about the immediate evils, the dangers that had surrounded her. But always, hovering beyond that, was the threat of *Eden*, the invincible city with endless resources, endless power.

Not so endless, maybe.

"Hey." Noah rose and spun the chair to face her before catching her hands in his. "By the time I'm done helping Dallas, no one will be able to touch you. Not while you're wearing his ink."

"What? No, that's not what I was thinking." Her gaze locked with his. "They're not infallible, and that means no one is. Especially not Fleming."

His fingers tightened. "That's what I'm counting on."

"Then why can't you see?" she asked desperately. "You don't need to go after Fleming, guns blazing. You can hurt him worse on your terms, doing what you do. *Thinking.*"

Noah's jaw clenched. "It's not that simple. I can't just live out in the open like a normal person. Fleming won't let me. My *only* chance at anything close to a life is taking him out."

"Is it? Or do you want to kill him so badly you can't see anything else?"

Noah hauled her closer, until she was straddling his thighs, practically in his lap. "I'll think about it, all right? For you, I'll think about it."

His proximity made her head spin, but she held her ground. "No, for *yourself.*"

He stroked up her arms and slid his hands into the loose strands of her hair. "It's the same thing. Until you get that, you won't get me."

Emma shivered. "Everything in your life can't be about me."

Tugging gently, he tilted her head back and pressed a kiss to the underside of her chin. "Why not?"

"Because..." There were a hundred damn good reasons—a *thousand*, even—but with his mouth on her skin, all that mattered was one. "Because you haven't said you'll stay."

"And that would make it okay?" His fingers tangled in her hair, pulling until her scalp tingled.

"It would make sense." Why deny that sort of all-encompassing emotion?

"That's not what I asked." He licked her pulse. Grazed her skin with his teeth. "It's obsessive. Possessive. Dangerous. Is that what you want?"

As if there was any other way to love in Sector Four. "O'Kanes don't do anything halfway, Noah. Especially not this."

Groaning, he forced her to meet his gaze. "Do you have any goddamn idea what you're saying? What you're *offering?*"

More than her body. Her heart, her soul, everything. But words would never convince him. "Give me one night to prove it to you. You get this thing done for Dallas, and I'll show you what it all means to me."

"One night?"

"Not some tits-and-ass setup so Dallas can show you how very luscious things are around here," she clarified. "The real shit. Fight night."

"Okay." His hands slipped from her hair, and she immediately missed the gentle pressure. "As long as you realize that if I show my face, I'll probably end up fighting. Too many people from Three want to take a swing at me."

He didn't exactly seem displeased by the prospect, so Emma smiled slowly and rubbed her thumb over his lower lip. "So climb in the cage and take a swing back."

His eyebrows lifted, and he smiled under her touch. "My turn to put on a show?"

"A little. But maybe also to see how O'Kanes celebrate victory."

"So sure I'm gonna win?"

"Lesson number one," she breathed, easing closer on his lap. "We always have faith in each other, and in our men."

He caught her thumb between his teeth and licked the pad, his eyes never leaving hers. She pushed farther, gliding her thumb over his tongue in a slow circle before pulling free. "Noah?"

"Yeah?" His voice was low, husky. His cock was hard

beneath her, straining at his fly, and she rocked against him.

Then she rose. "You have work to do."

Noah blinked. His mouth opened. Closed. When his lips parted again, a groan tumbled out. "Fuck, Emmy. You grew up *mean*."

His approving tone made protest and indignation unnecessary. "You like me. Admit it."

He grumbled as he swung back around to face the keyboard and screen, but a smile played around the edges of his mouth. "More every day, sunshine."

"Uh-huh." Emma melted back against the wall to watch him, his words echoing in her mind.

More every day.

Maybe it would be enough.

6

SECTOR FOUR'S FIGHT night was legendary.

And it was *real.* Emma hadn't been wrong about that. Noah had run into plenty of O'Kanes on the job, and he'd gotten an eyeful of how they played. But taken on its own it was fragmented data, a sub-process that told him nothing about the whole.

Fight night, on the other hand, was everything the O'Kanes stood for, distilled to the purity of their signature whiskey. Sex and violence, pride and challenge. Strength and protection. And standing next to Dallas O'Kane at the edge of the cage, Noah had the best seat in the house.

Well, maybe the second-best seat.

Most of the bare warehouse was standing room only, with a few battered tables and chairs around the edges. A few grizzled old men sat there with their drinks, taking bets and calling odds. But the space next to the makeshift bar held tiered stages covered in plush leather couches, and that was where the O'Kane women had gathered. They were screaming now, cheering as one of the O'Kanes beat an opponent into the rough cement. Noah had tried to pay attention to the fight, but his gaze kept drifting back to Emma. She was sleek and deadly tonight, in tiny leather shorts and a leather vest obviously invented by a sadist—some insane creation that snapped together beneath her tits and left so much of them bare that all he could think about was peeling it away to get his hands on her.

Or his mouth.

Or his dick.

"Lex told me everything, you know," Dallas drawled without warning, hauling Noah's gaze back to the leader of Sector Four.

Noah had figured she would, but it still cooled his lust. Dallas knew the truth, and no one would stop him if he tried to put Noah in a shallow grave. "Yeah? You want me gone?"

"Didn't say that." Dallas crossed beefy arms over his chest and watched the fight, but Noah had no doubt the man was aware of everything around him. "There's some ugly shit in your past. Doesn't make you special. But if you can't let it the hell go because she matters more, it makes you not fucking worthy."

Noah looked at Emma again. She caught the glance and smiled, tucking her hair behind her ear in a gesture he'd seen a hundred times. If he closed his eyes he could picture her, younger, softer, blushing as her fingers caught a stray lock of hair and smoothed it back from her face.

She'd always seen good in him, even when he was sure it wasn't there. He'd been equally sure she couldn't want the reality—the messy, fucked-up truth of his desires, the things he could barely admit to himself.

Sex and violence, pride and challenge. Strength and protection.

Possessiveness and submission.

Fuck, she'd been around the O'Kanes for three years now. She probably understood it all better than he did.

"Lennox." A tall, dark-haired man slammed back a whiskey and shoved his glass at a passing woman, earning himself a curse and a punch in the back. He ignored both. "You and me, in the cage."

It took a second for Noah to place the rough face, but when he did, a name followed, floating up from the data he'd assembled on the people of Sector Three. Andy Charles, a small-time player in the black-market trade between Sectors Two and Three.

Noah hadn't messed with the guy—but he'd refused to work for him. That was all it took to piss off a bastard like this, when they could almost taste the money Noah was cheating them out of by refusing to play ball. He'd beaten down plenty of guys like Andy Charles, usually in back alleys or broken-down warehouses, using the moves Cib had taught him to end the fights fast and dirty.

It would be different here, and not just because Emma was watching. Stepping into that cage meant stepping out of the shadows. If Fleming didn't already know where he was, he would by the end of the night. And he'd know that Noah was done hiding.

He glanced at Dallas. "You sure you want Mac Fleming gunning for me in your sector?"

Dallas snorted. "You think that'd be new? Mac Fleming's been gunning for me since I took over Sector Three. It'd be a nice change of pace if he did it out in the open."

The cage was empty now, the last fight over, and the burly man by the door was holding it half-open, watching Dallas expectantly.

Waiting.

"All right, then." Noah bent to tug at his boot laces, and Dallas must have made some sort of signal because the warehouse exploded in cheers and shouted bets.

He let it all blur into meaningless sound as he stripped down to his bare feet and jeans. Andy had already done the same and vaulted into the cage, leaving Noah to cast one final look at Emma.

She stared back at him as if the small army of cheering people around them didn't exist. Instead, the corner of her mouth tilted up in an almost-smile, and she winked at him.

God, how long had it been since he'd won Emma's trust with winks? He'd been harder then, growing brittle and wary from trying to shoulder his father's responsibilities without turning into him.

But she'd been worth softening his usual scowl with a wink, even though it looked ridiculous. *Especially* because it looked ridiculous. His face wasn't built for playful expressions, and the incongruity had always made her laugh.

A wink didn't look silly on her. It was sexy, sultry. Almost a promise, and one he was fucking well going to take her up on.

Soon.

The cage door clanged shut behind Noah, and with the lights blaring down on him, he couldn't pick her out of the shadows anymore. The world constricted to the metal cage and the man facing him, a scowl twisting his features.

Noah flexed his fingers and quirked an eyebrow. "Andy."

"Should have known you'd find your way here." Andy's scowl intensified. "Guess O'Kane has pockets deep enough for you to get your hands dirty, huh?"

"You never did get it, did you? Not everything's for sale."

"No?" He feinted a jab, then danced back. "Looks different from where I stand."

Of course it did, because he wasn't seeing a goddamn thing, not really. He'd never notice all the ways Four was different. He saw violent men and half-naked women, not the things that mattered. Strength in the women. Compassion in the men.

Banter was useless. He got it or he didn't, and it wasn't Noah's place to enlighten him or change his mind.

So he'd rearrange his face instead.

Flowing out of the way of another feint, Noah went in hard and fast, smashing his fist into Andy's gut. The roar from the crowd eclipsed the man's pained grunt, but he didn't let the blow throw him for long. He struck back, sloppy and rushed, aiming for Noah's temple.

Noah dodged the worst of it and took a glancing blow to the cheek—just enough to give him a nice bruise for Emma to fuss over later—but the contact put him inside the other man's guard.

His punch didn't miss.

His knuckles stung as he whipped Andy's head to the side, sending him stumbling back. He hit the metal bars, rebounded off, and charged Noah with a theatrical growl. Maybe it was supposed to intimidate him. If so, the man was an idiot, wasting time and breath making his intentions clear.

It only gave Noah time to think. Plan.

Bracing his weight, he let his opponent slam into his gut. A calculated step back, almost like a stumble, but Andy misjudged it. He'd lowered his head for the charge, planning to ram Noah over, but instead Noah slapped a hand to the back of the man's neck and smashed his knee up into his face.

Andy staggered, jerking his head back. Drops of blood hit the floor, raining down from his broken nose. "Son of a *bitch!*"

The sporting thing would be to give him a chance to recover, and Noah didn't give a shit. He hooked his foot behind the other man's calf and hauled him off balance, dragging him down with a hard shove to the chest. "Tap out, and I won't break anything else."

Andy struggled, swinging a wild, easily deflected blow at Noah's head. "Fuck you," he wheezed.

No, it wasn't sporting. But knocking Andy out before

his pride could get him in even deeper shit was mercy, so he did it with minimum fuss. Two hits and the bastard's eyes rolled back, leaving Noah free to rock to his feet as the noise started.

Screaming. *Cheering.* The crowd roared their disappointment and approval with equal vigor, and for a heartbeat Noah found himself frozen by the unfamiliar sensation of being the center of everyone's attention.

It was Jasper who opened the door, a rare smile transforming his stern face. "All right, Bruiser. You win. Get out so we can clean this mess up."

Noah tried to smile in return, but the expression wouldn't come. Not until he got away from all the attention, out of the spotlight and back into the shadows. Not while strangers jostled around him, slapping his bare shoulders and shouting words that flitted past him as an annoying buzz.

He didn't smile until he found *her*, standing on the edge of the floor in a circle of respectful space no doubt enforced by the O'Kane ink wrapped around her wrists.

Blood pounded in his ears as he forced past the first knot of admirers. People followed the path of his gaze and began to melt away, until an empty stretch of concrete lined with too-curious spectators was all that stood between him and Emma.

It was too fucking late. Fleming would know he had a weak spot by morning. By tomorrow night, he'd know it was Emma Cibulski.

Fuck, this moment had probably been in the back of Noah's head all along, buried in that dark place he refused to go, as if avoidance could make it disappear. It had played out so pretty—stick around, put her in just enough danger that leaving would make it worse. Maybe he was everything he'd always feared—selfish and obsessed and lying to himself about whether or not he'd ever planned on letting Emma go.

She was his. Good or bad, twisted or wrong, she was

his, and he closed the last few steps with a hungry groan, buried his bruised hands in her hair, and kissed her.

The crowd grew louder, but everything in Noah's world was Emma—her taste and her tongue and the fingers that clutched at his bare back, drawing him closer to the softness of her body.

She wanted him violent. Bloody. She wanted him demanding, and she was proving it, going sweet and supple beneath his hands, open and eager, giving him everything he'd never dreamed of allowing himself to want.

He growled against her mouth and caught her lower lip between his teeth. Emma shuddered, her hands gliding over his skin—ribs, sides, stomach—to rest on his belt buckle.

Three steps put her back against the wall. Wrapped in shadows, but not hidden—awareness of the crowd behind him prickled along Noah's bare spine as he braced his hands on either side of her head and licked her plump lower lip. "Something you want, Emmy?"

Her eyes were dark, glazed with pleasure already, as she traced her thumb over the warm leather of his belt. "I want to suck your dick," she murmured. "Right here, in front of everyone."

The words were so sweetly obscene that his brain stuttered. Oh, he wanted it. Wanted it for all the basest reasons, and he was tired of fighting.

Besides, before he promised to stick around, Emma should know who he really was.

He dipped his head to scrape his teeth over her jaw. Up, until he found the soft spot where her chin curved into her throat, and he set his teeth and sucked hard enough to leave a mark.

She whimpered and clutched the back of his head with the hand not lingering on his belt. "You have to say yes."

If she thought he'd stop at something as passive as *yes*, she was in for a surprise. He lifted his mouth to her ear. "Get on your knees, sunshine."

Her breath hitched, and she slid down the wall with a moan, pushing at his thighs until he took a step back, giving her room to kneel at his feet.

Christ, she looked good there.

And she knew it. There was no innocence in those dark eyes, no matter how big they were. There was hunger, strength, a reminder that the dominance games he'd played with the women in Five were rough and clumsy compared to the way the O'Kanes skated on the knife's edge between power and submission.

She could cut him to pieces, and yet his erection already strained his fly. "Take my cock out."

The buckle clicked as she worked it open, her movements fast and sure. His belt fell open, and she yanked at the buttons on his fly before dragging his jeans and his underwear down to free him.

Emma exhaled on a shaky sigh and looked up, both hands clenched in the loosened denim of his jeans. She didn't touch him—not yet.

Not without a command.

"Good girl," he whispered, dropping one hand to cup her cheek. He swiveled his thumb to press against her mouth, drunk on the anticipation strung out between them. "Is this what you wanted to show me?"

"Yes." She whispered the word against his thumb as goose bumps rose on her arms and her nipples tightened beneath the thin leather she wore.

Good. Resisting the temptation to push into her mouth, he gripped his shaft, stroking once and shuddering when her gaze followed his fingers. The crown was already slick, and it satisfied something uncivilized inside him to trace the tip over her lips.

She opened her mouth. Her tongue darted out, lush and pink, and grazed the head of his cock. A quick caress, over in an instant, and he might have imagined it except for the flash of animal satisfaction that had him growling. "Again."

She blinked innocently, an expression belied by the wicked smile that followed. "Again?"

Noah gritted his teeth. "Put your tongue on my cock."

Only three snaps held her tiny leather vest closed, and she popped the first one free as she complied, lapping at his crown with short, teasing strokes.

Too slow. He'd been hard before she got on her knees, and the liquid need sliding through his veins left no room for practiced seduction. He released his shaft and sank his fingers into her hair instead. "If you take out your tits, I'll think you want me to come all over them."

Emma froze with her fingers on the second snap. "Tease."

He laughed. He couldn't help it. "Sunshine, don't think for a second there's a single place in or on your body I wouldn't love to come."

Her eyes flashed fire, and she fisted her hand around the base of his shaft with a low, drawn-out moan. "Dirty," she whispered, then drew her tongue in a slow circle around the head of his cock.

Shuddering, he tightened his grip in her hair, holding her in place as he rocked forward, pressing between her lips and into the wet warmth of her mouth. "Not as dirty as the things I'll do to you before I get to that point."

She moaned again, the sound vibrating through him in delicious tingles. She looked up, her gaze locking with his, wordlessly begging him to continue.

So he did, focusing on the plea in her eyes to distract himself from the dizzy pleasure as she sucked him. "I never had all the fancy cuffs and chains O'Kane was showing off at that party the other night, so I learned how to improvise. Your arms folded behind your back and my belt around them... With your cheek on the mattress and your ass in the air, you wouldn't be able to get away from my tongue."

Emma jerked, her hand tightening around his shaft and sliding back as she took him deeper.

Yeah, she liked that image as much as he did.

He twisted his fingers in her hair in silent warning, tugging her back until he could thrust shallowly into her mouth. "I think you'd try to get away," he whispered. "I think you'd like it when I stopped you."

She started to bob forward again, but he held tight. She gasped, straining for a heartbeat before relaxing with a gentle sigh, and a new languor softened her movements as she rubbed her head against his hand.

How could anyone compare grudging acquiescence to *this*, the heady moment when a powerful woman trusted you enough to let herself be powerless? It was like his first shot of O'Kane whiskey after a lifetime of rotgut liquor, so good it ruined him.

There was no going back. Nothing would ever be this good, this sweet.

No one could ever be her.

He withdrew, ignoring her whimper of protest, and taunted them both by stilling with her lips wrapped around just the head of his cock. "Maybe I'll get one of those bars with the leather straps that buckle around your thighs. You'd be able to wiggle all you wanted, and I wouldn't have to hold you open. I can think of better uses for my hands."

Emma sucked hard before releasing him with a *pop*. "And you called me mean."

He grinned at her. "Hey, if you can't handle what you're getting into..."

"For you?" Her gaze was solemn. "I've been waiting for years."

Levity bled into a fresh wave of hunger so intense that it shoved him across that final line. He shook as the truth tore from him, a promise or an admission or maybe a plea for forgiveness. "Me too. *Christ*, me too."

Emma rose in a rush and clawed at his chest as her mouth found his in a desperate, bruising kiss. He ripped open the snaps on those tiny leather shorts, and then he had his hands on her bare ass, and he didn't care if every goddamn person in the warehouse lined up to watch them because *nothing* was worth another second of not being inside her.

He hoisted her with his fingers under her thighs, only distantly aware of the wetness that greeted his fingers. She was as turned on as he was, and that was all the encouragement he needed to go fast and rough, shoving into her hard enough to slam her back against the wall.

She cried out, as sharp and sweet as her nails digging into his back. Her legs locked around his hips, and she shivered against him.

"You've always been mine," he said, rasping the words in her ear. They felt almost as good as the slick tightness of her pussy as it clenched around him. "Always."

"Say it—" The words melted into a shudder as she arched off the wall. "Say it again."

Not just accepting. *Encouraging*, and he was lost, driving into her again and again, because he wouldn't be deep enough until she felt as desperate and helpless as he did. "Always mine, sunshine. Your mind and your heart—" He rolled into her, tilting her hips until he could grind against her clit. "Your perfect fucking body. *Mine.*"

Her whimpers turned into choked moans and then into incoherent pleas. "You have to—please. Please, Noah—*God*, you have to—" She clamped even tighter around him, her whole body poised and trembling on the edge of ecstasy.

Getting a hand between them meant losing the press of her skin against his. Instead, he thrust harder, rolling his hips in tiny circles that worked her clit, and trusted his words to shove her over the brink. "Tell me I can keep you, and I'll stay."

"Yes." She ground out the word between clenched teeth as her trembling turned to a full-body shudder. "Yes—fuck, *Noah*—"

She came, gasping his name for everyone to hear, and

the knowledge that they could twisted pleasure into something hot and dangerous as he resumed his quick, hard pace. He wasn't just riding her orgasm to his own. He was claiming her in the most primal way possible, marking his ownership like a rutting fucking beast with the blood and sweat from the cage still slicking his skin.

And she clung to him, moaning and whimpering as each thrust pushed her back toward the precipice. Her nails raked his back as she came again, quieter but more intense, her pussy drawing him deeper with every rippling wave of pleasure.

He gave in, gave her everything, driving home one last time as he buried his face in her neck. "Christ, Em."

"I love you." She said it with her mouth close to his ear, a whisper just for him, and he didn't deserve any of this. Not her body or her mind—and especially not her perfect fucking heart.

"Emmy likes you. She really, really likes you, man. Hell. I think she might love you."

Just a ghost, a nightmare, and Dallas was right. If he couldn't carry the weight of the past for both of them, he would never be worthy of her.

He wanted to be worthy. But wanting didn't make it effortless, and the words stuck in his throat, came out cracked and raw. "I love you, too."

She heard the lie. Not his emotions—loving her was the only thing that had ever come easy—but the one he'd sworn never to tell. It was the only explanation for the way her smile faltered, for the gentle hand on his cheek and her dark, questing gaze.

I'm sorry. "I never thought I'd say that to anyone," he whispered, covering the lie with more truth. "I never thought I'd want to."

That brought back a smile that lit her whole face. "Practice," she murmured. "That's all you need."

If the guilt didn't eat him alive first.

7

EMMA WOKE FROM a dreamless sleep to the soft rasp of paper sliding over carpet. She saw it instantly, a vague square of white against the darkness—a note, slipped under her door. A summons, maybe, some directive from Dallas or Lex.

She closed her eyes again and snuggled deeper under the covers. Noah's arm was draped across her waist, heavy and comforting, and he'd nestled his face against her shoulder. She wanted to roll on top of him and wake him with a kiss, not climb out of bed and read her note. But it might be important—vital, even—so she groaned softly and swung her feet to the floor.

Noah grumbled behind her, but she'd swept up the paper and turned before his eyes cracked open. "What's that?"

Noah's name was written across the outside in Dallas's bold script. "It's for you."

He blinked. "A note? A goddamn treasure trove of tech sitting above his storage room, and Dallas O'Kane passes *notes?*"

She switched on the dimmest lamp at her bedside, dropped to sit beside him, and handed him the folded paper. "Can't hack a note."

Judging by the perplexed look on his face, it had never occurred to him. He snorted as he rolled to his back. "I guess not, but most people are lazy. They'll take the chance if it saves a minute or two."

"Not Dallas. He's *traditional.*" She sang the word as she walked two fingers teasingly up Noah's chest. "What does he want?"

Noah unfolded the note and studied it, his brow furrowing. "Information."

"What kind?"

Still frowning, he showed her the words.

Lennox,

I need the Council's file on illegal bootlegging inside of Eden.

If you can get it.

Dallas had scrawled *O'Kane* at the bottom, and Emma snorted. Perfectly worded as a challenge more than anything else, and guaranteed to elicit a reaction. "You can get it...but will you?"

"Do you know why he wants it?"

There was no point in hiding the truth. "Someone's been selling counterfeit O'Kane liquor. It has to be someone with the experience to distill, so Dallas probably figures whoever it is has had run-ins with the military police."

Noah nodded. "And finding out whether I can get onto Eden's servers would be a bonus."

"Mmm, undoubtedly."

He plucked the note from her hands and tumbled her back to the bed, stretching out above her with a too-serious expression. "It's a test. Are you still sure you want me to pass it?"

There it was again, the same flash of hesitation she'd seen in the fight warehouse. A cold knot coalesced in her stomach, and she swallowed hard before asking carefully, "Is something wrong, Noah?"

"Trust is hard." He traced a fingertip over her brow before sweeping a strand of hair from her forehead. "How much do you trust Dallas?"

She stared down at the O'Kane cuffs encircling her wrists. "I wouldn't have these if I didn't trust him more than damn near anyone else."

He followed her gaze. "Good enough," he said after a moment, then dropped a kiss to her forehead before rolling away. "I can get what he needs, but I'll have to go to Three."

"I'll go with you." The words escaped without thought, instinctive and automatic.

Noah froze on the edge of the bed, his shoulders tense. "It's dangerous, Em. I know O'Kane's starting to clean the place up, but it still isn't safe."

"All the more reason you need someone to watch your back."

He turned to study her wrists, lingering on the ink. "You've got a weapon?"

She kept her pistol in her nightstand, so it took her only seconds to retrieve it. "We don't go out unarmed, not anymore."

"Smart." Noah capitulated with another smile, leaning in to touch her chin. "Dress in something sturdy. We're going underground."

He wasn't fucking kidding.

At first it was a regular trip through Three—navigating broken streets and dodging piles of trash, though the mess had been cleaned up considerably since

Dallas's takeover. But then Noah led her into a crumbling building with only half a roof, and Emma started to wonder whether the dangers of the trip had anything to do with other people at all.

They climbed down a broken staircase that had been patched together with what looked like a ladder from a fire escape, and Noah handed her a small flashlight. It was the only way to see, because the boarded-up windows had vanished, leaving only brick, concrete, and earth to line the walls.

They were underground.

Noah shoved a desk and a few rusty folding chairs aside, revealing a heavy steel door with an inactive control pad next to it. While she held the flashlight, he popped open a switchblade and pried off the cover. "This is the scenic route," he said, pulling a miniature solar battery pack from his pocket. "But it bypasses the sewers, and trust me. You want to avoid those."

"Yeah, no shit." She'd worn the sturdiest clothes she owned—jeans, boots, and a duster made of heavy leather—but even those wouldn't stand up to a traipse through sewage.

The wires inside the control panel had already been stripped. Noah fiddled for a moment, twisting them with the wires from the battery pack. The face of the panel lit up, illuminating his furrowed brow and narrowed eyes as the door squealed open. "Welcome to my neighborhood."

Emma stepped into the tunnel and stared at the seemingly impenetrable darkness until the clang of the steel door swinging shut startled her.

She'd heard rumors about these tunnels. Hardly a month went by without a new story of some treasure hunter getting caught in a cave-in, sometimes whole goddamn groups of them. Dead in an instant.

But Noah wouldn't have brought her here if he didn't think he could get her out again, so she tightened her grip around her flashlight and followed him down the endless tunnel.

"Here." He grasped her free hand and tugged her to the left, and when she swung the flashlight around, she caught sight of another steel door and a block-letter sign.

He repeated the trick with the battery pack, muttering curses under his breath until the panel flared to life. He pressed his palm to a screen beneath, and the door whispered open. Lights flickered on in the hallway beyond, and Noah grinned. "That was the hardest part, after finding the damn place. Figuring out how to steal power without tipping Eden off to it."

"How did you?"

"I tricked their computers into thinking this bunker was part of Sector Five." He retrieved the battery pack and ushered her through the door before closing it from the inside, leaving no trace of them behind. "Figured it was only fair for Fleming to pay for my resources."

Another door lay in front of them, this one with a round handle that looked like a steering wheel. A blast door, the kind Emma had seen in pre-Flare movies about wars and fallout shelters. The handle creaked with a metallic shriek as Noah turned it, and he pulled it open to reveal a row of metal rungs set into the concrete—a ladder, leading down into another corridor, brightly lit and far more inviting than the last dozen.

She climbed down and then stopped awkwardly. It felt like trespassing, so she waited until he joined her. "This is it?" she asked softly. "Your home?"

"Yeah." He settled his hand at the small of her back and prodded her around the corner, into a tiny kitchen. It was open to the rest of the room, which held more furniture—a couch, a couple of plush chairs, and a dining room table covered in partially assembled electronics and scattered scraps of paper. "It took me almost a year to find it. I was starting to think my father had made the whole thing up."

"Guess not." She shoved her hands in her back pockets

and looked around. "It's like it was built for the end of the world."

Warm arms slid around her, and Noah buried his face in her hair. "It was, in a way. But the world ended a little ahead of schedule."

Second-guessing the past was a quick trip to crazy town, but just this once, she couldn't help wondering how different things might have been if she'd stayed with him. "If you had known how to find this place, would you have brought me here with you?" She turned, because she had to see his face when he answered. "Did you want to?"

He framed her face, his touch gentle. Reverent. "Yes. I was too old and you were too young and there were a million reasons it was selfish and stupid, but sometimes I'm selfish and stupid."

A different life—and a different Emma. Aside from the four years they'd lost, she didn't want that. "It doesn't matter. I love who I am. I love being an O'Kane. And as long as you're with me now, that's all I care about."

"I wanted you," he repeated in a softer voice, touching his thumb to her lower lip. "But I like you better like this. I never wanted you to need me, and now you don't."

"Not like you mean." Being this close to him was sparking the now-familiar buzz, arousal flowing through her, and she wrapped her arms around his neck. "I need you in better ways."

"The best ones," he agreed, and kissed her.

He started slow, but every stroke of his tongue was deeper, hotter, than the last. Emma fell into him, and the room fell away—until she realized they were moving, and the backs of her legs hit something soft.

The couch.

But he didn't stop kissing her. Not as his hands slid up her body and under her coat, urging it off her shoulders and down her arms. Not as he skated those clever fingers under her shirt, warm and tauntingly gentle on her sides, her belly, her breasts.

Too gentle. She tried to kiss him harder, but he lifted one iron hand to her jaw and held her still while he started all over again.

Emma whimpered.

"Shh." He raised his head far enough to meet her eyes as his free hand drew circles across her skin, inching closer and closer to her breast. "Do you trust me?"

The question brought a laugh bubbling up, disbelief and amusement. "Of course I do. I'm just *really* fucking turned on." His shirt was in the way, so she reached for it.

He closed his fingers around her wrist, as unyielding as steel. "Emma. Do you trust me?"

She stopped and swallowed—hard. Not an idle question, or even a reassurance, but the first step down a path they'd only flirted with up until now. A little hair pulling, a command here and there—

This was different. A serious question that deserved a serious answer.

"You said last night that I'm yours, all of me." She nodded slowly. "I am. I trust you."

He smiled and kissed her one last time, a quick brush of lips and a stinging tease of teeth before he stepped back and dropped his hands to his belt. "Take off your clothes. All of them."

Shoes first, then she stripped off her shirt so she could watch him unbuckle his belt. "Is this some alpha-bastard thing? Because I'm in your domain now?"

"Maybe." He tugged at the buckle, leather hissing over denim as he freed it from one loop at a time. "Did the girls in Five tell you that I like to be methodical?"

"*Intense* is usually how they put it."

His lips quirked. "That wasn't intense," he murmured, catching her arm. He spun her so fast she stumbled, and he steadied her against his chest as his lips brushed her temple. "That was just sex and control. But I've never had any fucking self-control when it comes to you. I want everything."

Warmth from his body—and his words—suffused her skin, sliding down her spine to join the wet heat already gathering in her pussy. "What does that mean? Everything?"

Instead of responding, he guided her hands behind her back. And he *was* methodical, repositioning her until her arms were folded on top of each other, the fingers of each hand brushing the opposite wrist.

The belt was cool compared to his touch, smooth leather bearing down into her skin as he looped it around. "Tell me if it's too tight."

Her voice came out breathless, feathery. "No, it's—" A shiver knocked her teeth together. "It's all right."

She heard the soft click of the buckle and the rustle of fabric. He pressed against her again, his chest bare this time. One warm hand splayed large across her abdomen as the other slid under her chin, angling her head back toward his. "Trust and love. That's everything."

Even in her most self-indulgent fantasies, he'd never looked at her like this, like *trust* and *love* were words that only meant *Emma*. "Noah..."

He tugged open the button on her jeans. "Yeah?"

She couldn't remember what she'd planned to say, but that was okay. It couldn't be more important than his hand slipping into her pants, or his mouth so close to hers. "Please."

His lips brushed hers. Lingered. He traced the edge of her panties with one fingertip. "Are you wet?"

She fought the urge to stretch up on her tiptoes, to arch closer to his hand. "Yes."

"Good." It was almost a groan, and her world upended. He lifted her, spinning them both in a dizzy circle before dropping her to the couch on her back. His tense, precise calm shattered as he hooked his hands in her jeans and underwear and dragged them free of her body in a tangle that ended up flung across the kitchen counter.

Before she could draw in a breath he hauled her upright, shoved her thighs wide, and sank to the floor between them. The belt around her wrists snagged on the bottom of the cushioned back of the couch, leaving her immobilized, her back arched.

She tried to shift position, but Noah gripped her waist, his thumbs moving in soothing circles. "I like you like this, with your tits thrust out and your legs spread wide. I can see all the ways you're hungry for me. Your hard nipples and your slick pussy."

She was acutely aware of all the ways she was exposed, and it took superhuman effort not to fidget or close her eyes to block out the intensity of his stare. Instead, she watched him as she rocked her hips experimentally, and moaned when she slid a few inches across the now-wet, slippery surface.

Groaning, Noah gripped her thighs, pushing them wider. "Stay like this," he warned as he stroked his fingers over her pussy. "If you move too much, I'll have to stop licking your clit and find some rope."

She froze, her heart pounding.

"That's right." So soft, so warm. It was Noah's smile, the one he saved for her, but so much rawer like this, with his thumbs spreading her outer lips, baring her completely.

Then he bent his mouth to her pussy, his tongue swiping a hot, merciless line straight to her clit. The breath she'd been holding exploded out of her on a helpless cry. And helpless, that's exactly what she was—bound and trapped by his hands and his mouth, by his desire.

She never wanted to be anywhere else.

He repeated the motion, his gaze lifting to catch hers as he lingered this time, flicking the tip of his tongue across her clit. "What part got you this hot, this fast? Tell me."

Oh God. "The way—" The words wobbled, and she steadied herself. "The way you kiss me."

Another groan, one that rumbled against her as he

licked his way lower. "Because you're mine."

"Yes." She had to move somehow, so she braced her clenched hands on the couch and arched her hips more fully against his mouth.

If he noticed, he didn't say anything. He was too busy working his way back up to tongue her piercing. "You're mine, but that's not why you sucked my cock in front of half the sector last night, is it? You wanted them to know I'm *yours*."

Just hearing the words out loud sent a bolt of pleasure rocketing up her spine. "That's what I learned," she rasped. "All I know. It goes both ways."

"Show me." The tip of one finger circled her entrance before pushing in, and she was so wet, so *ready*, that it glided deep. He groaned and added another, working into her body as he growled a command against her pussy. "Come on my tongue."

His fingers were blunt and impossibly wide. She'd seen them fly across a keyboard and float over reactive screens with ease, but she'd never imagined that he could play her body just as skillfully, dragging her toward the edge with such dizzying speed that the rest of her could barely catch up.

Then he drew her clit between his lips, sucking with an aroused groan.

She shattered, bucking up with a shriek. With every wave of ecstasy, she clenched tight around his unyielding fingers, so tight that he sent her spinning straight into a second orgasm with a clever twist of his wrist. Emma couldn't breathe, could only feel, until sensation over-whelmed her and she begged, *begged*—

"Shh." He whispered it against her ear, and she had no idea how he'd gotten there. His fingers remained inside her, broad and strong and still, but even as she gasped in a helpless breath, he rocked them gently, setting off another wave of shudders. "Stay with me, sunshine. I'm not done with you yet."

She blinked, but the world was swimming. "Noah."

"Emma." He lifted his head, hovering over her with a soft smile. "I love how fast you come. How hard. You know your own body."

Because shame and modesty weren't prized or celebrated in Sector Four. But he seemed just as into filthy sex, and it made her curious. "Don't you know yours?"

"I know it just fine. Accepting is the hard part. Believing that you want the same things." His thumb grazed her clit, and she hissed in a breath. "I love this. I love making you feel good."

"But?"

He eased his fingers free, but only for a heartbeat before they were pressing back into her. Three this time, too big and too much, and his gaze stayed locked on hers as he twisted and rocked, edging them deeper. "Some of the ways I want to make you feel good aren't as pretty."

It took mere moments for the pain to yield to pleasure. Emma exhaled on a moan, but the hesitation in Noah's eyes lingered, and only the truth would erase it. "Noelle would have four fingers in me already," she murmured. "And she'd be telling Jasper to hurry the fuck up with the lube."

Noah groaned against her cheek, and his groan turned into a kiss, and then a bite. His teeth left a stinging trail of fire down her throat until they closed around the tip of her nipple.

She clamped her lips together to hold back a moan, but then he swung his thumb up to circle her clit, and the noise escaped—pleading, desperate. Wetness and warmth enclosed her nipple as he sucked it into his mouth, tugging so hard that, any other time, it would have crossed the line into pain.

But not now, like this. So close, with his fingers filling her, fast and a little rough, with no hesitation. His thumb stroked out a rhythm he'd already memorized, with no respite at all from the blazing pleasure. Every quick revolution bumped the barbell she wore, back and forth, over and over, until the world shrank to Noah—his hand on and inside her pussy, his tongue on her nipple, his body stretched over hers, hot and protective—and she came again.

Hard. Almost violent, twisting beneath him until he had to hold her down, trapping her under the weight of his body so there was no escape from the sensation, the heat, and the giddy relief.

"*Fuck*, Emma—" His body vanished and she was floating, rising up off the couch. She savored a few moments cradled against the warmth of his chest before he lowered her to the floor and bent her forward over the arm of the sofa.

Her cheek hit the cushion, and she struggled to catch her breath as he stroked her spine. "Tell me you want this."

The closest she could get to reaching for him was flexing her hands. "I want it."

"My cock?"

"Your cock," she panted. "*Yes*."

"This is my fantasy. Making you come on my fingers and face until you're begging for it." A zipper rasped open, and the metal teeth dug into her skin as he bent over her, bracing one hand on the couch above her head. He traced her mouth with the other, his fingers still slippery from her body. "What does that say about me? You're tied up and helpless and I can ride you as fast and hard as I want, but your body isn't enough. I need everything."

She bit his fingertips, then soothed them with her tongue. "Give it to me. Everything. You'll get it back, you know you will."

He left a trail of kisses down her spine as he eased back, soft and sweet and swallowed by the rush of anticipation when she finally, *finally* felt his cock gliding against her pussy.

Just that, and she bit her lip for as long as she could,

but then the ridge around the head of his cock grazed her clit, and a whimper escaped. "Noah—"

He drove into her—fast, hard. Merciless. Emma muffled a cry against the couch cushion and clenched her eyes shut, but light exploded behind her lids when he did it again, and again.

And again.

"Feel me," he growled, fingers digging into her hips, angling them so there was no escape, no reprieve. "Feel everything."

"I do." It came out in a whisper, and she didn't know if he heard her, but surely he knew. She always felt him, even when he was missing from her life—a hole in her heart where Noah should have been.

He shuddered, one hand sliding up past her arms to her shoulder. His fingers tangled in her hair, hauling her head back, and a shudder ripped through her, too. "Is this how you like it? Hard and rough?"

"Yes." Every thrust rammed her hips against the smooth vinyl arm of the couch, and she could still taste herself from his fingers on her lips. It was raw and loud and so, so real. Every bit of sensation cascaded into a flame that unfurled inside her, fed by the harsh, trembling thread of desire in his voice.

He ground in a circle, forcing her to feel his girth, how deep he could get. "You like my cock shoving into you?"

"*Yes*," she choked out.

Groaning, he withdrew until the head of his cock barely pressed against her. "Say it," he whispered roughly, and the need in his voice was so desperate, so *naked*—

Even bound and trembling and physically helpless, she had the power to crush him.

"I need you, because I love you." So close, and she already felt like she was floating. Free. "Just like this."

Something inside him snapped. He dragged her up against his body, one steely arm crossing her chest, supporting her weight as his hand curled over her shoulder to anchor her in place.

And he had to, because the next thrust was hard. Wild. He slammed into her, growling in her ear, the sound eclipsing the slap of his hips against hers as he fucked her. Fell into her.

Loved her.

With her back so sharply arched, every thrust hit her G-spot—but it wouldn't have mattered if he'd withdrawn and started whispering in her ear, because it was the force, the sheer desire behind it, that drove her over the edge. She shook apart, reckless and helpless and lost to the moment.

That didn't matter, either. Noah would hold her.

"Emma." It was the one thing that existed beyond her pleasure, his voice chanting her name as he rode her release to his own, and she was still drifting away when he shuddered and stilled with a final whisper. "I love you."

There was no dark reservation behind the words now, just Noah, and tears pricked her eyes. "I know."

For an endless moment he stayed like that, clutching her against him with trembling arms as his breath fell fast and hot on her cheek. When he finally moved, it was only to coax her a few unsteady steps back. He dropped into a chair and tugged her with him, his fingers fumbling at the belt until it slithered free.

"Are you okay?" he asked, rubbing his hands over her arms.

"Hmm?" It made no sense, because *okay* was such a weak word for this.

She felt the curve of his lips when he kissed the back of her shoulder. "Good answer."

Part of her wanted to stay like that, to ignore the reason they'd come there in the first place. "How long will it take to find what Dallas needs?"

"Here, with all my equipment? Not long."

He was stroking her bare skin, and Emma's eyes tried to flutter shut. She snapped them open. "If you're worried about being jumped here in Three, it seems safest to get the fuck out before dark."

"I know." He caught her chin and tilted her head back, until his lips touched the corner of her mouth. "It's just hard to let you go."

Her chest ached, like her heart was too small to contain the rush of joy at his words. "I'll be right here."

He kissed her, quick and abrupt, pulling back as if he didn't trust himself not to fall into her. "That had better be a promise, sunshine."

"Always."

P ARANOIA HAD DRIVEN Noah to park far from the entrance to the tunnels, and sometimes paranoia paid off.

The bastards were staking out his bike.

They didn't even try to hide. Three familiar figures milled around the motorcycle he'd taken from Dallas's garage. The fourth man was sitting on it, fiddling with levers as a cigarette dangled from his lips. He tapped a finger against the speedometer and muttered something that made one of the other men laugh, rough and ugly.

James Hobbs could say any damn thing, no matter how inane, and the idiots clustered around him would laugh, eager to curry favor. Hobbs was one of Fleming's lieutenants, a man with just enough power and influence to support his chosen lifestyle of greed and violence.

Not a smart man, not by Noah's standards. But he was cunning and vicious, and the sight of him shattered

Noah's desperate illusions.

Less than twenty-four hours after Noah had come out of hiding, Fleming had sent one of his top men into Dallas's territory, violating every agreement between the sector leaders—not to mention common fucking sense.

This wasn't over. It would *never* be over.

"Hobbs." Emma's jaw clenched. "Trouble, after all."

Noah had two guns and a chance to claim the high ground—and the element of surprise. Decent odds of getting through to bring back help, as long as he didn't get distracted. "Do you remember the way back to the bunker?"

But she was already drawing her own pistol. "You've got to be shitting me."

He struggled to keep his face stern and cool as he grabbed her wrist. "Don't even think about it. You're going someplace safe."

"Thought you said no place was safe as long as they were after you."

"The middle of a gunfight is arguably *less* safe." He leaned into her, backing her against the crumbling brick wall, and he couldn't even lie to himself. This could be the last time he touched her. The last time the words hovering on his tongue would be true. "You said you were mine."

"I also said it goes both ways." She laid her hand on his cheek. "I'm not leaving you, Noah. If there's gonna be a fight, I'll be *here*. Watching your back."

No one had, not since Cib had gone off the rails. So many years of being alone, exhausted, and if having her was too good to be true, having her like this was some kind of cracked fantasy. A woman, a lover, a *partner—*

Exactly what Dallas O'Kane had.

Closing his eyes briefly, he pressed his forehead to hers. "How good of a shot are you?"

"Let's just say you don't want to piss me off."

Wanting to smile made him crazy, but he couldn't help it. She was deadly and she could take care of herself, and if shit went sideways and he couldn't be a part of the life she was going to build...

She'd be okay. Emmaline Cibulski didn't need rescu-ing.

"All right," he whispered, straightening. "They won't kill me, not here. I can go out—"

"*We*," she corrected, wrapping her hand around his.

He squeezed her hand. "Then stick close, and if it goes bad, go for Hobbs. He's a misogynist fuck who won't see you coming." And if something happened to him, the greatest danger to her would already be dead.

Hobbs didn't rise as they walked out into the street, just took a long drag off his cigarette. "Speak of the devil," he said lazily. "This your bike, Lennox?"

"Nope." Two of the fuckers were eyeing Emma, and Noah consoled himself with a silent promise to end them before they could touch her. "You can take it if you want, but it's your head if Dallas O'Kane wonders why you were in his territory, stealing from him."

"Not here to take anything that belongs to O'Kane." He paused, filling his silence with a lingering appraisal of both Noah and Emma. "Mac's been looking for you."

"Has he?"

"Mmm. But you already knew that."

Noah let the corner of his mouth curl up just a little, the perfect bored, condescending smile. "I wasn't sure. He hadn't sent anyone capable of actually finding me. Until now."

"You'd never thrown in with Dallas O'Kane before," he answered distractedly, then pointed at Emma. "I know you."

She stiffened, and Noah slid between them, breaking Hobbs's line of sight. "You know me," he said firmly. "You really think I've thrown my lot behind a goddamn bootleg-ger? At least Mac deals in medicine along with the drugs."

"Desperate times." He snapped his fingers. "Shit. That's Cibulski's sister, isn't it?"

His palm itched. It took every scrap of control not to go for a gun now, not to blow off Hobbs's head before he could say the wrong thing, spill a secret that would tear any and all comfort from Emma's memories of the past. "That's an O'Kane," he said instead. "I'm sure you all know what that means."

"Noah Lennox—not such a saint after all." Hobbs laughed as he swung his leg over the bike and rose. "Settle a bet for me. How much did you pay for her?"

Brick after brick of lies and half-truths, and James kicked through them with seven words. He was glad Emma was behind him now, glad he wouldn't have to see her face when she realized the truth.

And Hobbs would tell her. Noah could see it in his eyes, the animal instinct of having sniffed out a weak spot. The pleasure at being able to exploit it. "Don't do this," he said softly. "I'll end you, I swear to fucking God, James."

The man's grin widened, turned wolfish. "Cib was a piece of shit, but he drove a hard bargain. He was asking twenty grand, cash, last I heard."

It had started at five. That was the number Cib had floated in the nightmare Noah couldn't stop reliving. Five thousand dollars, and Emma would be his. It wasn't even some dirtbag plan to whore her out for the night, because Cib hadn't been sober enough to think long-term. He'd been strung out and desperate, intent on pawning the one family heirloom he had left.

Five thousand bucks, and Noah would own his sister forever.

Noah had shut him down, only to learn a week later that the five grand included a friendly discount. Open bidding started at ten thousand, and it became clear Cib wouldn't stop until he'd put money in his pocket.

In the end, Noah almost wished he'd taken the original deal. It had cost him twenty-five thousand to buy Emma's freedom, and he'd paid it, thinking he was buying Cib's, too. Another week, and he could have gotten them both out of there, out of the sectors and away from the drugs fucking up his best friend's head.

He didn't get a week. Cib turned up dead three days later, his corpse ceremoniously seated at the fucking kitchen table for Emma to find—a message and a warning.

Hobbs interrupted his horrified reverie. "Come on, Lennox. Answer the question. How fucking much?"

Emma spoke, her voice soft and deadly. "You don't listen very well, do you? He said to shut your face."

Hobbs's grin vanished. "You've got a smart mouth, bitch."

"You don't." Emma glanced at the other men, who'd gone on alert, shifting from lazy positions to watch closely. "Go tell Fleming he's too late. If he fucks with Noah, he fucks with the O'Kanes."

Hobbs turned a hard gaze on Noah. "Nah. I don't think so."

Noah had to move fast. The three other men were still milling about, silent shadows wearing brass knuckles and intimidating scowls. No guns, because Hobbs wouldn't have trusted them at his back, not when Noah might have offered them a sweet deal in exchange for a traitor's cheap shot. That was how he'd always operated—by turning his enemies against one another.

Not this time. This time he wanted blood.

He lunged to the side as he pulled his pistol, drawing Hobbs's attention with him. The man drew his weapon, but Emma was quicker. She squeezed off a round, and Hobbs stumbled backwards and fell.

The closest other man swung at Noah. He took the hit on the left shoulder and spun around, ignoring the throbbing pain in favor of getting a better angle.

No hesitation. No mercy. This close, a head shot was easy, final. One bullet, and the back of the man's head splattered all over the brick wall behind him. Noah spun and put a second bullet into another man's chest.

Emma fired again, and the third man—the biggest—

grunted as blood bloomed on his shoulder. He hit Noah, driving him to the cracked pavement.

The impact knocked his gun out of his hand, and it skittered across the pavement to land in a pile of debris. Out of reach, pinned as he was beneath his attacker's weight. Twisting, Noah ground his thumb into the wound on the man's shoulder, eliciting a pained shout that ended in a grunt as he slammed his hands into Noah's throat.

Emma yelled his name a split second before swooping down on the injured man with a wicked-looking knife in her hand. She stabbed him in the shoulder and then went flying as he reared back far enough for Noah to roll free.

He came up with his second gun and put two bullets in the bastard's chest. He toppled in what felt like slow motion, a dreamy silence rent by Emma's furious shriek.

Noah knew what had happened before he turned—a warning tingle at the back of his head, a clenching in his gut—

Hobbs, his face pale and streaked with blood, held Emma crushed to his chest, her own knife pressed to the vulnerable column of her throat. She struggled, and the blade bit deeper, deep enough to draw a gasp—and a bright red line of blood.

No nightmare compared to this.

"Let her go," Noah said, amazed that he sounded so calm, so cool. He was shaking inside, rage and terror twisting up until there was no room left for anything else, no reason and no compassion.

"Why?" Hobbs took a step back, dragging Emma along.

"Because I can do worse than end you." The knife sliced into Emma's skin, and every drop of blood felt like failure. He had to get her away from this—away from *him*, if that was what it took. "Let her go, and I'll come back to Five with you."

Her eyes widened. "Noah—"

Hobbs ignored her. He coughed out a laugh, and flecks

of red splattered Emma's shirt. "I'm not going back, Lennox. But I can take her with me."

And he would, out of sheer spite. One last *fuck you* to the world and to Noah for sending him out of it, and there'd be nothing left. No brightness, no sunshine, no joy—

Noah steadied his hands to risk a head shot, but the distinctive flick of a switchblade interrupted him. Emma's free arm, the one not bracing against the knife at her throat, jerked back. At the same time, she twisted, gripping Hobbs's wrist and wrenching it out at an unnatural angle.

The knife clattered to their feet, and Emma kicked it away. But she didn't even have to bother, because Hobbs stood there, stock-still, and looked down at the wicked black handle protruding from his belly.

Yeah, Emmaline Cibulski could fucking well take care of herself.

It didn't stop Noah from shooting Hobbs, just in case.

The man slammed to the asphalt, lifeless, Emma's knife still sticking out of his gut. Noah ignored him like he'd ignored the rest of the trash, striding across the space between them to reach for Emma. "Are you—?"

She jerked away before he could touch her. "No."

She was bleeding, but he didn't think the cut on her throat was the cause for the pain behind the words. And he wanted to pile more on top of it, to swear it wasn't as bad as it sounded, that Hobbs had twisted the truth—

There was only one thing he *could* say. "I never thought I owned you."

That froze the pain, turned it to ice in her eyes. "What did you say?"

"I never—" His stomach twisted, and he clenched his fists. No excuses justified his failure. Anything he said now would be about making himself feel better. "Cib loved you," he said instead. "The drugs fucked him up. That's what they do."

Her hands squeezed into fists, and for one second, No-ah was sure she'd slap him, so sure he could already feel the crack of her palm across his cheek.

She hit him with a whisper instead. "Do you even hear yourself? So fucking desperate to make sure I know you did everything you could, that you did everything right. Well, fuck you, okay?" Her voice rose. "I need a minute to wrap my head around the fact that my brother sold me like a goddamn whore, and no one ever bothered to tell me, so *fuck you*."

It would have hurt less if she'd slapped him. If she'd *stabbed* him. But she was right, so Noah gritted his teeth and stayed silent.

She stood there, staring at him. "The drugs fucked him up," she finally echoed in a rasp. "I buy that. But what's your excuse?"

"My excuse?"

"Cib figured he could sell me. And you figured you could buy me." She held both hands out to her sides. "Save me from my life, right? I'm sure it was all very noble."

It didn't sound noble, not with the lash of disdain under her words. "It wasn't like that. God, Em—I wasn't buying you, I was buying *time*."

"What did it change?" Her voice thickened, and the first tears spilled down her cheeks. "My brother was a fighter, and he loved me. If he was hawking me to his buddies like a fucking secondhand guitar, then he was dead already. Shit just hadn't caught up to him yet."

Or maybe it was one more way Noah had failed—by not getting him out fast enough. Maybe he should have damned the debts, packed them up, run as far and as fast as possible, and fuck the consequences. "What else could I do?"

"That's the wrong damn question, Noah."

"Are you going to stand there bleeding while I try to guess the right one?" He reached for the hem of his shirt. "At least let me—"

"*No.*"

If he touched her, she'd probably pull another knife. "I did what I could, okay? It was fucked up and selfish and wrong, but money was the only thing I had to fix it with."

"That's the problem, and you don't even get it, do you? You still don't *get it.*" Emma turned and headed for the opposite end of the alley—and the street. "Let me know when you figure it out."

Worry propelled him another two steps after her. "Wait, you can't just walk back alone."

"The hell I can't."

Her voice made it clear this wasn't a battle he could win, but it was so hard to stop fighting. "At least take the fucking bike."

She kept walking, right out of his life.

It took everything he had in him to let her go.

E MMA HATED HERSELF for crying, but she couldn't help it. Steam from the shower billowed around her as she leaned against the tile, fighting the ugly sobs that threatened to tear free of her throat. It didn't seem real yet, walking away from Noah Lennox. He'd been so many of her firsts—her first crush, her first love.

Maybe it was only fitting that he be her first broken heart, too.

The hot spray stung her neck, so she climbed out, toweled off, and gingerly applied a thin layer of med-gel over the shallow slice across her throat. She should have done it first thing, but she'd only wanted to hide in the shower and let the water wash away her tears.

Her bed creaked, and she hated herself anew for hoping it was Noah, that he'd followed her, that he'd come back—

It was Lex, perched on the edge of the mattress, with

Dallas standing beside her.

His gaze jumped straight to her throat, eyes narrow-ing. "Who?"

Her hand rose automatically to cover the wound, and Emma forced herself to relax. "Some asshole from Five, one of Fleming's enforcers. Don't worry, he's dead."

"And Lennox?"

She looked away. "I'm assuming he's fine."

Lex rose. "Are you all right?"

How the hell could she answer that when she could barely feel anything beyond a sick, burning knot in her gut? "Did you know?"

It had to be bad for Dallas's eyes to soften like that. "You're gonna need to be more specific, darling."

To her credit, Lex didn't try to deflect. Instead, she muttered a curse and sighed. "I told Lennox to keep his mouth shut. Ordered him to, even, so if you want to be mad, here I am."

As if he'd ever planned on telling her. Emma snorted. "That's real self-sacrificing of you. It's also bullshit."

Dallas laid a hand on Lex's shoulder and kept his gaze on Emma. "*Did* he tell you?"

"No." That would involve Noah stepping back, treating her like an adult by not trying to protect her constantly. "I found out from the guy who almost slit my throat instead. That was much easier to take than hearing it from a friend."

"Careful." It only took three of Dallas's ground-devouring steps to cross the space between them. He lifted her face with one gentle finger under her chin and studied the wound. "No, this isn't how it should have come out. But I told him to hold his damn tongue because I needed to know what sort of man he was."

"He's—" Her voice cracked, and she squeezed her eyes shut.

Lex made a soft noise and rubbed her bare shoulder. "Oh, honey."

Dallas slid his fingers around to the back of Emma's neck, his touch soothing and affectionate. Safe. "Hard truths are simple until it's time to lay them on the people we love. I didn't want him dumping his guilt on you and splitting."

"He wouldn't." Instead, he'd be leaving her to face all those inevitable hard truths, dazed and unsteady. Unprepared.

"Would or wouldn't, it's not about him. Not right now, not with us."

"I know." The painful knot in her throat migrated to her chest. "My brother *sold me*."

"Yeah." Lex tugged her down to sit on the end of the bed and wrapped both arms around her. "It sucks. And I don't give a damn if he *is* dead, you get mad, Emma. Because that was shitty."

"No fucking excuse." Dallas sighed and crouched in front of her. "But it was never about you, and I know you know that. That shit Fleming cooks up is toxic. Doesn't just make people addicts, it makes them crazy."

"Yeah." The worst part was that she understood that. Cib never would have done it if he'd been in his right mind. What really hurt was all the years she'd spent not knowing what had happened or why or *how*— "Do you know what happened?"

"From what I've heard?" Lex hesitated. "He took on a delivery for Fleming, but instead of selling the drugs—"

"He took them himself," Emma finished flatly.

"He took them," Lex confirmed, pulling her closer. "Then he had to pay up."

Amazing how still her hands were, when inside, Emma was dying. "I blamed myself. I thought he'd had a run-in with someone because of his job, because he was trying to support me. I thought if only I hadn't been there, dragging him down, he would have been all right."

"Ah, love." Dallas's hands were huge and covered hers completely. "That's bullshit. Fleming was the weight around his ankles, but he tied it on his damn self. Don't you ever think otherwise."

Easy for him to say. "I might not have assumed it was my fault if anyone had bothered to tell me the truth."

"Fair enough." He kissed her forehead and rocked to his feet. "One more question. Does Lennox need to stay the fuck away from this sector?"

"No." Hating Noah would be straightforward, simple. Better than feeling betrayed by his lack of faith in her strength. "No, he and I are square."

"Emma..."

"He belongs here, Dallas." Nothing less than the truth. "You know it."

He grunted. "We'll see. Lex?"

"Go on." She twisted a wet lock of Emma's hair around her finger until the door slammed behind Dallas, then she shook her head. "He needs to hit something. Probably not Noah, though."

Emma laughed helplessly and grimaced as she gestured to her cut. "Don't make me giggle. It hurts."

"In more ways than one," Lex murmured. "Look, honey. I could say a lot of stuff right now, and none of it would help, not one damn bit. So let me just tell you that I don't know how you feel, not exactly...but I've come close to a lot of it."

Lex knew about being sold, and Lex knew about betrayal. How much did she know about heartbreak? "I gave him everything."

"Everything?"

"Mind, body, and soul."

"And heart." Lex sighed and stroked her hair. "If you gave him that, you know it's not that simple to take it back. Walking away is hard as hell."

She didn't *want* to walk, but how was she supposed to move past the knowledge that she'd been floating through the past four years, living a lie? And, Christ—what if Noah's guilt ran deeper than even he realized, and the connection he felt to her was because of it?

She wished for numbness now, but the only thing she couldn't feel was her lips as she mumbled, "I guess I need to talk to him."

"Later," Lex said firmly. "Right now, we worry about you, baby girl. That's all."

Relief left her weak as she leaned in to Lex's comforting embrace. She'd be strong in front of Noah—she'd be *steel*—but here...

Here, she could afford to cry, just a little.

The bar in Sector Three was no Broken Circle, but it was a lot nicer than it had been before Dallas and his people took over and started cleaning things up. Under the previous owner, Noah would have expected to get jumped for his spare cash within five minutes of crossing the threshold.

If the man approaching Noah's table kicked his ass, it wouldn't be for anything as trivial as money. And he had it coming.

Bren slid into a chair and raised both eyebrows. "Is there a reason you dragged me all the way over here, Lennox?"

Because he didn't trust himself anywhere near Emma, not with desperate loss shredding him up from the inside out. But he couldn't admit that to Bren, so he slid the data chip across the table instead. "Everything your boss needs."

Bren pocketed the chip with a nod. "You didn't answer my question."

That was the problem with hardcore Special Tasks soldiers, present or former. Once they locked on to a target, it was impossible to distract them. "Did Six ever tell you about what I did?"

"You mean handing her all my military evaluation

vids?"

It had felt righteous at the time. *Right*. Six had barely known Noah, but he'd felt like he knew her all too well. She represented the worst of what could have happened to Emma—a tough girl sweet-talked by the criminal leader of Sector Three, and too tangled up in his bullshit to break free by the time he started to hurt her.

So when Six ended up with Dallas O'Kane, with *Bren*, it had seemed like the decent thing to do—make sure she wouldn't get blindsided a second time.

What a smug fucking hypocrite Noah was. "I thought I was giving her what she needed. Knowledge. Turns out, it's easier to tell other people's secrets than your own."

"No shit." One of the dancers, a pink-haired girl in platform heels and not much else, set a drink in front of Bren, and he picked it up. "You were right not to come to Four. I wouldn't say Dallas is gunning for you, but he sure wouldn't mind fucking your face up a little."

"There's a long line for the privilege." The need to ask about Emma throbbed in Noah's chest, but he ignored it. "I shouldn't have brought her with me. Dallas brushed it off, but I knew Fleming would come at me."

"What, the fight?" Bren downed his drink. "I doubt that has much to do with our fearless leader's desire to punch the shit out of you."

"It should," Noah retorted, and even self-preservation couldn't keep the anger out of his voice. "I painted a target on her back, and now I have to figure out how to fix that."

"A smart man uses his skills to his best advantage." Bren slanted him a look. "I thought you were a smart man."

It was an echo of Emma's plea for him to use his brain, and that drew a morbid smile. "I've always been a smart man, but I guess I lack inspiration."

"So get inspired. Get *motivated*." Bren rose and shoved his hands in his jacket pockets. "Get it done, and make it right."

He'd gotten inspired the moment that knife touched Emma's throat, but the plan hadn't come until he'd forced himself to watch her walk away. A crazy plan. A fucking reckless one that might end with a bullet between his eyes.

But if it worked out, she'd be free. And so would he.

Noah stood, as well. "If what I have planned works, O'Kane will forgive me. If it doesn't..."

"It better. Don't make her cry again."

Better to make Emma cry than to leave her with a second lifetime of regrets. Of *guilt*. "If it doesn't," he repeated softly, "tell her I did it for me. That I was tired of running."

Bren hesitated, then nodded slowly. "I'll tell her you did what you had to do. For yourself."

"And take care of her, Donnelly. Promise me."

"Emma can take care of herself."

Physically, maybe. He believed that now. But in every other way... If the persistent ache in his formerly numb heart was anything to go by, the O'Kanes were the most vulnerable bastards around. There was a certain safety in not feeling. In hopelessness. No disappointment, no regret, just dull relief that you were still breathing when the sun set.

Joy and hope were better. Brighter. But they made loss cut so damn deep. "Take care of her heart."

Bren started for the door before calling back over his shoulder. "She's an O'Kane. That makes her family."

Family. Not always a rousing endorsement, especially for Emma. But this time, Noah would believe in it. He had to believe, and then he had to forget. He wasn't an actor, but he didn't need to lie for this, just tell the worst parts of the truths he'd tried to hide from all those years.

Freedom wouldn't come cheap, but she was worth it.

Mac Fleming didn't look evil.

He seemed pleasant enough on the outside. Hand-some, Noah supposed, though women seemed equally transfixed by his aura of power—and his money. He sat behind a polished desk, his expensive suit just rumpled enough to suggest he'd been interrupted in the middle of something.

Probably banging his latest mistress. Mac had a wife and family tucked away on the edge of the sector, but Noah had spent over two decades running the tech for his factories without hearing Fleming speak about them more than a handful of times.

"Noah," he said casually, an unmistakable thread of glee wreathing the word. "What a pleasant surprise. I've looked everywhere for you, and here you come—walking into my office."

Noah didn't bother to hide his disdain. He didn't need to. "It only seemed right to tell you in person that Hobbs isn't coming back."

"Now that isn't so much a surprise." Fleming pulled a cigar from a humidor on his desk and snipped the end. "Who did him in? Was it you or Cibulski's sister?"

Hearing her name on Fleming's lips was chilling, but it worked for the game. "So you know she's there."

Fleming laughed. "She's not exactly incognito, shaking her tits in O'Kane's club, is she? Didn't even change her name."

Noah's hands fisted, and he embraced the anger. Let it play across his face, a true emotion he used to spin the lie that followed. "O'Kane's a lot less subtle than you are. When making her dance didn't draw me out, he tattooed his fucking mark on her."

Fleming sparked an antique lighter and puffed at his cigar as he lit it. "Did he? That's your property, not his."

"I know," he ground out, and *goddamn*, he shouldn't have been worried about summoning enough outraged fury. The real challenge would be in not going for Fleming's throat. "He thought he could control me through her. Even you were never that stupid."

"Bitches come and go." Fleming said it solemnly, like he was laying down some kind of universal, philosophical truth, then followed it with a pointed look. "What's your play, Lennox? And what do you want from me?"

"The same thing I've always wanted." It was hard to say it like this, to a man like Fleming. The truth, in all its sad, twisted glory. "I want her. And I want out."

"So you want protection."

"You really think you can protect me from O'Kane if I take one of his women?"

The man slammed his hand down on the desk hard enough to rattle everything on it. "Dallas O'Kane does not rule this sector, and he doesn't rule me!"

For a heartbeat, Noah wondered if he'd pushed too far. Fleming had always been insecure about the power he'd inherited from his father—especially compared to a self-made man like Dallas. But Noah needed him angry.

Vengeful.

He took a step back—calculated, because he couldn't fake fear or respect, but he could show retreat. "I'm just saying O'Kane is strong. We both know it. But maybe I could do something to change that."

That quickly, Fleming's ire faded, replaced by a satisfied smile. "If O'Kane's so dangerous, playing him could be deadly. You prepared for that?"

Ego would be this bastard's downfall. Smiling, Noah tweaked it. Buttered him up. "As dangerous as walking in here to make demands?"

"That remains to be seen." But Fleming gestured to the chair across the wide desk from him. "Have a seat and tell me what you have in mind."

10

EMMA HURT, SO she did what she always did. She threw herself into her art.

She'd already designed three sheets of flash and had moved on to yet another new back piece for Ace—one he'd let her ink this time, maybe—when the bell on the door jingled. But whoever it was also knocked, so she dropped her pen and leaned around the partition. "Come back in a few—"

Noah.

He stood there, so stern and silent, but the blankness in his gaze that had scared her on that first night was gone. He looked sad and a little nervous, but he looked *alive*. A person instead of a ghost.

It hit her in the chest, the uncertainty clouding his features, and she had to swallow hard just to speak. "Did you figure it out?"

"I don't know," he admitted. "But I started using my

head, so maybe there's still hope."

"Yeah?" She leaned over the back of the tattoo chair—guarded, this time. Slow, because tumbling headfirst after Noah Lennox had gotten her hurt already.

"Yeah." He took a deep breath and exhaled, and she knew she wasn't going to like the words that came next. "I went to see Mac Fleming."

By some miracle, she kept her breathing and expression even. "Did you tell him I said hi?"

Noah didn't smile, didn't flinch. "I told him Dallas O'Kane marked you to control me. And he believed it, because it's what he was planning to do."

"Okay. So you're—what, now? Working for Fleming again?"

Noah shoved a hand through his hair. "That's what he thinks. I convinced him I'd help him take down Dallas in exchange for leaving the two of us alone."

And instead, he'd be working the other side of the fence—handing Dallas intel on Fleming's operations and plays, no doubt. "Good for you."

"It wasn't hard. I just had to tell him the truth." Noah lowered his voice to a rough whisper. "I told him I've always wanted you."

She had to physically keep herself from covering her ears, so maybe she *was* a child, after all. "Stop. Please."

"Em—" He clenched his hands. "I'm not asking for anything. Not forgiveness, not a chance. I just needed to say it, because you were right. I decided what was best for you and did it, over and over again, and I pretended it was all selfless because I didn't want to be the guy who wanted you and bought you and got to keep you."

He *should* have been asking for forgiveness, because she'd promised him more than her heart. She'd promised him this, the moment where even if he hurt her, he could fix it by understanding.

She gripped the back of the tattoo chair. "For four years, Noah, I blamed myself for Cib's death. And now, here I am, with all of his mistakes slapping me in the face. I can barely wrap my head around it."

"Do you have questions?"

Only one really mattered—the same one she'd asked Lex. Only Noah would know it all, the truth, not just rumor filtered from sector to sector. "Tell me what he said."

Noah didn't have to think, or struggle to remember. He closed his eyes, and the words had the too-quick cadence of recitation. "He said he was in some trouble, that he'd gotten rolled on a sector run and needed cash. He said that he'd seen the way I look at you, and that you really, really liked me. That you might even love me. He said I could have you—forever—for five thousand dollars."

It didn't sound real, delivered in that carefully detached tone. "Five thousand," she echoed. What had to be going on in your mind to put a price on a human life in the first place, much less your baby sister's?

"I don't know what he was playing at," Noah said softly. "He knew I wouldn't let him sell you to one of Fleming's men, so maybe the bidding was just a bluff. Maybe he just didn't know how to ask for help, and I was trying so hard to do the right thing that I couldn't hear him screaming for it."

And maybe by then Cib had been so desperate for a short-term fix to his very deadly problems that the ends had justified the means. "I don't know what to think. Part of me feels like I should hate him, but I don't." She was pissed, sure, but even the heat of that emotion paled next to her insurmountable sadness.

"I'm sorry, Em. That it happened, that I didn't tell you..." He met her gaze, held it. "You were young and scared, and that seemed like a good enough reason to protect you from the truth. But you're not either of those things anymore. You're a woman, you're tough, and you deserve everything."

Every word battered at the fragile walls she'd constructed, threatening to rip them down. "Do I deserve a partner? Someone who'll stand beside me and help me, not try to shield me from everything? Because that's that I want, Noah. It's all I ever wanted."

The hope in his eyes was almost painful. "Even if I'm still tangled up with Fleming? Spying for Dallas isn't going to be easy or safe."

"I'm an O'Kane," she answered simply. If he didn't get it by now, he might not. Ever.

But Noah nodded, as if that was all the response he'd wanted. "And I'm yours. Not because you need me, but because I need you. A woman who has my back."

But she couldn't resist challenging the words. "Not because you feel responsible for me? Or worse, *sorry* for me?"

Noah laughed, rusty and a little wild. "Guilt you can lay on me, sunshine, but pity? No. Most people in this world have sadder stories than yours, with no O'Kane family to dust them off and hug it better. And the best I could have done for you?" He waved a hand, taking in the art studio. "Nothing like this. You found your home without me, and it's a damn good one."

Tears stung her eyes and hung thick in her throat. "I still want you here, though," she admitted softly. "If you want to share it with me."

He took two steps and jerked to an abrupt stop, his hands shaking until he gripped his belt, as if to hide it. "I want you. Here or in Three, I don't give a fuck, as long as you're there. At my back and in my bed."

"Because you love me." The same eager hope burning in his eyes laced her words, too, and she didn't give a damn. She wanted him to know, wanted the *world* to know. "Say it."

He reached past her and plucked up one of the blue tracing markers from her desk. He jerked the top off with his teeth and offered it to her. "You say it for me. In ink."

Emma stared down at his outstretched arm for a few

frozen moments, then glided the marker over his forearm, slowly forming her name in swooping, trembling lines. "You love me," she repeated.

"I love you." He held out his other arm, offering his body as her canvas. "I'm yours."

Her breath seized in her lungs.

This time, she drew a heart—but not bound, like the one she'd inked on his chest. Free, unfettered, ringed with block letters that again spelled out her name. "I can keep going, but I'll need more skin."

He moved fast, catching the hem of his shirt and hauling it over his head. "You can have anything you want."

"Anything?"

"Name it, sunshine."

She pressed the marker into his hand and tugged her own shirt over her head.

His throat worked as he swallowed. "I'm not as good an artist as you are."

"I don't care." She framed his face with her hands, skating her fingertips lightly over the scruff on his jaw. She'd memorized his face already, every line, and she'd do it all over again—a hundred times, a thousand. "Mark me, Noah."

His gaze swept down to settle on the bare stretch of skin along her collarbone, and the tip of the marker tickled as he wrote his name in careful letters. After a moment's hesitation he added two more words.

Noah Lennox loves me.

Warmth slipped through her veins and turned to heat at his proximity. "Did you mean it? That you'd say it with ink?"

"Yes." He tossed aside the marker and traced the words he'd written with his fingertip. "That's what O'Kanes do, isn't it?"

The need pounding through her exploded, obliterating the last of her self-control. She kissed him, but it wasn't enough. He'd never understand how deep and how hard she loved him, not from a kiss, so she raked her nails over his skin as she dragged him closer.

She couldn't bear to break contact, not even to speak, so she whispered against his lips. "You're staying with me?"

"I'm yours," he said again, but his fingers had wound their way into her hair, twisting tight. "If you're not ready to be mine, I'll wait."

The thought was unbearable. "No—now."

He groaned and kissed her again, licking her lips until she parted them. He was still methodical, still determined, but the hungry edge in his kiss was so close to the surface.

It wouldn't take much to shatter his self-control, and Emma wanted it more than breathing. His belt clicked under her fingers, and she tugged at the ends of his open belt until his hips ground against hers and he hissed out a breath.

"Now?" He gripped her hips and lifted her up. "Christ, Emma, I swear I didn't come here just to get my dick in you..."

Too goddamn bad, because it was all she could think about now. "Tell me." Her voice was almost embarrassingly low, husky. "Tell me what you want. The truth."

He shuddered. "I want to watch you come riding my cock."

The tattoo chair was right behind them. Emma flipped up the arms to get them out of the way and pushed Noah down onto the black vinyl. She watched him as she kicked off her shoes and tugged her jeans open with one hand, riveted by the sight of his muscles flexing as he unzipped his pants.

He had his cock out by the time she was naked, but when he hauled her astride his lap, he didn't drive into her. He held her hips to his, his shaft grinding against her pussy, and licked a hot path down her throat. "Touch yourself. Your tits. Please."

"My—" The words dissipated as he rocked his hips,

and the head of his cock nudged her clit. The intensity of the slick glide—somehow lazy and desperate, all at once—stole her voice.

So she moved instead, cupping her breasts for him. His tongue swept out, hot and wet, circling her nipple. Then he sucked it into his mouth, and his hands kept clutching, kept *moving*, rolling her against him, urging her to rub her clit along his shaft.

The chair rocked, and Emma shivered. "Noah—"

"Now?" He tightened his grip, lifting her. "Is this what you want?"

"Please." She didn't have to memorize him anymore, or lock this moment into her brain forever, because he was *hers*.

He shifted until his cock was poised at her entrance, and then he let gravity pull her down. Even though she was inescapably turned on, impossibly *wet*, he still filled her with an aching stretch that left her trembling on the edge.

His head thumped against the seat, and he closed his eyes and gripped her hips. "Christ, don't move. You feel too fucking good."

"Not even like this?" Emma braced her toes on the floor and eased up until only the head of his cock remained inside her, and she pressed her thumb between his lips as she hovered over him.

Growling, he closed his teeth, trapping her hand as *his* thumb slid through her folds. His eyes popped open, blatant challenge in his gaze as he circled and stroked, working toward her clit.

The contact shot up her spine like a shock, and Emma shuddered. The liquid heat gathering in her lower body flared, making her legs shake as his thumb circled again. The heat didn't subside, just swept over her in a sudden, sharp orgasm, the kind that came and went in a heart-beat, left you trembling.

She drove down against him, crying out as her clenching muscles gave way to the sheer size of him. He bit off a curse, thrusting up into her, harder, *deeper*, and his voice broke through the blood pounding in her ears. "Fuck yes, I love it when you come all over me. Let me feel it. Let me feel *you*."

There was no hiding her pleasure from him, even if she'd wanted to. Instead, she embraced it, winding her arms around his neck as another wave of ecstasy gripped her. "Don't stop, Noah."

"Never. *Never*." He dragged her to meet his next thrust, crashing their bodies together. "You can mark every inch of me."

She already had, years ago, in ways no one could see but that were just as real, just as permanent. There was no part of him he hadn't yielded to her, heart and soul, past and future.

Fantasy and truth.

They moved faster, their bodies picking up the pace as they strove for the peak. It had never been so important to Emma to tip over it together, two people locked together as one.

She clutched his shoulders, her hands slipping on his damp skin until she dug her fingernails in for purchase, eliciting a hiss that turned into a groan. "With me," she panted. "Come with me—"

He kissed her, moaning her name against her lips as the first shudders took him, and Emma let go, let the pulsing of his body inside hers drag her over the edge too. She rode him through their orgasms, blinded to anything in the whole fucking world that wasn't *Noah*.

Finally, he stilled beneath her, and she came to rest—her forehead to his cheek, his heart pounding against her chest.

"Fucking hell." He smoothed her hair back with shaking fingers before turning to kiss her cheek. "All those years wasted, when I could have been loving you."

The answer was easy, obvious. "You were."

He choked on a laugh and coaxed her head back, urging her to meet his eyes. "Fine, then. All those wasted years, I could have been being loved."

"You were that, too." Her smile faded. "I always knew. Sometimes, I tried to tell myself you were just being nice to Cib's little sister, but when you talked to me... On some level, I knew better."

"You were a smart, sweet girl." He kissed the corner of her mouth, teasing her with flicks of his tongue and nips until she smiled again. "But you're a filthy-hot, tough, amazing woman. You're a partner. *My* partner."

"It won't be easy." Then again, things worth having never were.

Noah laughed against her mouth, and it was the first time in so many years that she'd heard him laugh, really laugh, all joy and no shadows. "Fuck easy. I want wild. I want you."

Laughter, love, and a lover who didn't need to be her savior, didn't need her helpless and at his mercy. Everything she'd ever wanted, in the one man she'd always craved.

Emma tucked her face into the hollow of his shoulder and smiled. "Then you have me."

ABOUT KIT

Kit Rocha is actually two people—Bree & Donna, best friends who are living the dream. They get paid to work in their pajamas, talk on the phone, and write down all the stories they used to make up in their heads.

They also write paranormal romance as Moira Rogers.

the **BEYOND** series

Beyond Shame
October 2012
Beyond Control
March 2013
Beyond Pain
August 2013
Beyond Temptation
February 2014
Beyond Jealousy
March 2014
Beyond Solitude
April 2014
Beyond Addiction
coming fall 2014

FIND KIT ON:

FB: http://www.facebook.com/thebrokencircle
Twitter: @kitrocha
Web: http:///www.kitrocha.com